Summer Juice

Summer Juice

Wayyback Wynn

13th & Joan Publishing

First Edition Printed, July 2020

Library of Congress Cataloging-in-Publication Data has been applied for.

ISBN: 978-1-953156-01-3

Dedication

The highest praise goes out to God for blessing me with seeds of creativity that I can now say is sprouting from this book. A lot of hard work and obstacles came from writing this book and yet, he saw me through. I want to thank the unconditional love, sacrifice, and support of my family. I love you, Mom (Donna). I love you, Dad (Todd). And I love you, Sierra. We all we got; and with all that I do, I just want to make y'all proud. Outside of my family, I appreciate the growth and push from the best institutions in the land: Stephenson High School and Vanderbilt University. Every person who was my teacher/professor and coach wanted me to do better, and I thank them. Last, but not least, I thank my friend circles. My best friends, #3Live ,Da Crew, La Familia, my Vandy brothas, mentors, etc. You all keep me going and inspire me to keep being great. I love y'all. Rest in Power to Mr. David Williams and George Floyd. Thank you, 13th & Joan Publishing House. And now, I have a story to tell.

Epigraph

Moments of nostalgia can prove to be the keys to happiness.

Table of Contents

Preface

Let me take you back to the golden years of the 2000s. The only reason why those are the golden years is because they were my childhood years. A time period where "bling" was so popular that you did all you could to fake it to you make it. Instead of asking Mom to give me a quarter for the gumball machine, I would ask for a dollar to get the silver chain out of the other dispensary. Sometimes she would give me a dollar; most of the time, she didn't.

Baggy clothes and big white tees were the style then. Pine Ridge Elementary School had a dress code of red polo shirts and khaki pants Monday through Thursday; but once Friday came, the Sean John fits would come out of the closet and set the tone. The Air Force Ones would take flight as soon as I stepped in school. Plus, the gold chain I would "borrow" from my mom's jewelry collection was the sprinkles on top. The only thing is that my mom would always buy high roller jeans like it was the '70s. As soon as she would say, "Have a good day, Jonathan," I would wave and unbuckle my belt a little, so the jeans could look more loose-and yes, I did sag...Please forgive me.

So many memories I visualize and laugh at from that time, but I think the best memory, that holds the most weight, is growing up in the neighborhood of Riverbirch Trace, a street where everybody knew everybody-well, at least in the cul de sac. You had my family's house, the central spot for kids to play the PlayStation and receive popsicles every hot day; next door to me was Mr. Richard, your typical elderly man, who just wanted the kids and me to stay off his yard when we played hide-n-seek. On the other side of our house was the Unknowns, the people you never see all year. All you would see is their cars parked or gone. Their house was the type you had to play Ding-Dong Ditch on, because they never came to the door. You had Calvin and Steve across from me, always ringing the doorbell for me to come play outside. We could be coming back from church and they would run up the driveway, asking if it was okay to come outside. Graham and Keysia were right next to them, before they moved to San Francisco. They would play with us too, but at reasonable times of the week, not on a Sunday. Then you had Ms. Esperanza, a Hispanic lady, who was always gardening in the front yard. I believe I saw exotic flowers for the first time through her garden. Roses, cherry blossoms, gerberas, and violets. Every year was a new flower. A bouquet display all spring and summer. The one thing I noticed about Ms. Esperanza is that every time we were outside playing in the cul de sac, she was outside gardening. Plus, she had this Chihuahua to let us know too every time I walked through her yard. One day I went over there to help her and hopefully make a little money. While I was shoveling dirt for her garden bed, she told me a little about harvest season and how she stayed on top of it. She would plant in the fall and harvest in the spring and summer. Her logic made sense because when winter came, her house would look vacated. Rarely did I see her in the winter. Once late April came, she was back outside fixing her garden. Her cycle of waiting and tending her plants reminded me of my childhood in the neighborhood. Early fall through the winter, kids were planted in the schools or the house. Once late spring came, kids were out of the ground, blossomed, ripened for freedom and looking forward to summer break, which meant playing outside all day, summer camp, summer vacation, and all of the above in my neighborhood--which is what gave the neighborhood life and made my childhood memorable. The sun would pigment the colors of the red-brick houses and plants, the vibrancy of summertime BBQs and Saturday morning yard work sizzled into the air. The serenity of children playing and music coming out of the trunk of Mr. Steve's (Calvin & Steve's father) car gave the neighborhood a soundtrack. It made me not want to stay inside as a kid because it was a horizon with the best view that you couldn't get anywhere else.

In 2007, we moved to a different house. In the moment, I didn't understand, but I do now, looking back on how the recession affected most families. It hurt me. I was devastated to leave the house, the neighborhood that meant so much to me. I knew then that my childhood was over. Some things do not last forever. The last time I was back in that neighborhood was April 2018. I finished my undergraduate studies at Vanderbilt University in December 2017. From then on, I worked at Smoothie King and trained for my school Pro Day, a football showcase to present my athletic skills in front of NFL team scouts. That day changed my life. NFL scouts saw my talent and immeasurables. They clocked me with a good time in the 40-yard dash. The same 40-yard dashes I would do in the neighborhood with Calvin and Steve to see who was the fastest. Scouts measured me with a good vertical jump. The same vertical jump I would do to try to touch the basketball rim in the neighborhood. The coaches, who did my drills, saw the athleticism that had been growing since the neighborhood tackle-football games in the cul de sac. After that grand occasion, I had teams calling, wanting to get to know me.

As the NFL draft drew closer, I knew I wanted to go back to my parents' house and celebrate with them. Plus, invite my day-one friends over as well. We had a BBQ, and family came over for the joyous day. During that moment, I was chill with the hype of the draft. Too chill, actually. Friends would ask, "How do you feel?" I would say that I was good, not really understanding the significance of the opportunity to play in the NFL. I think I understood when I went back to the old neighborhood the Sunday of the draft weekend. I drove into the subdivision and pulled up, just in awe of how different it looked. It was sunny that day, too, yet it didn't have the same aesthetic, same appeal, same attraction. The garden was gone. The new owners must have replaced it with bushes. My old house had new pieces in the yard. Kids were not outside along the street. The scenery of what I loved was gone. The one thing that was a capsule to my memory was the power box, where we would take a break in between games, figure out the next thing to do, or just chill and talk.

The funny thing about the box is that that was where I would talk about playing in the NFL. Michael Vick was our boy for the Atlanta Falcons, so we would talk about playing just like him, scoring touchdowns and juking every player out. Then, after talking about it, we would do it, either against ourselves or against another neighborhood crew.

Seeing the power box made me understand the importance of the weekend. I said to my friends that I would be in the NFL one day, and now I am.

When we made plans to do something, for the most part, we did it. One time we needed money to get the new NBA Street game that came out during that time. Because we knew our parents would not give us the money for the game, we would knock on neighbors' doors and offer to work for money. If you ask a kid to do that now, the probability of them doing it would not be as high as it was before. They will resort to other ways that may require less work and may be a shortcut route. Coming up with Summer Juice came in the midst of going into the league and wondering if everything was going to work out. It was a transitional period where I was excited to be entering the real world, and yet wishing I could be Peter Pan for one more year.

If I had a DeLorean to travel back in time, it would be to my childhood days. The days where life was simple. I had so much energy as a kid and I had few worries as well. Fast forward 15 years later and there is so much anxiety and doubt of not making it or not fulfilling the pressures of a high performance business; yet I knew writing would be my passion outside of football. Summer Juice became my coping mechanism to handle the madness that was life at the time.

I knew my first story would be a coming-of-age one because I love that genre. The way my dad would tell me his stories as a kid made me feel like I was there, so I knew I had to start there. Whenever I had time after practice, I made sure to write in my journal to continue the story. It became a consistent process during mid-May through the later part of July. The funny thing is that I read the rough draft version of Summer Juice on Instagram Live for my viewers. I called it my "Short Story Special." The inspiration of the idea came from PBS television shows such as Reading Rainbow and Mr. Rogers' Neighborhood.

Writing and telling the story, I knew I had to tap into my style, which is Wayyback Wynn. A style that has old school flavor along with the style and swag of my generation. Original to my heart and authentic from my experiences. After I read it aloud, people loved the story, but I hope you love it with your personal voice.

Preface

Introduction

Do you ever wish Sunday could be every day of the week? Some days I do. It's not the thought of attending church or eating a good Sunday dinner, but the feeling of everything being at ease and relaxed, while still reflective and motivating. Imagine that every day. Your life's soundtrack is the vibe of a smooth gospel song, silky, with the church organ touch. On the Sunday mornings I attend church, I like to play my favorite gospel playlist, filled with songs that give me the Holy Spirit, and have Jesus chauffeur me to the sanctuary.

One of the songs that uplifts me whenever it plays is "It's Working" by William Murphy. If you listen to the song, you would not think the song was called "It's Working"; you would believe the title was, "This is My Season," because the lyrics plant in your mind how this is the time for you to seek out the purpose God has for you, to where it will work out for your good.

As soon as the song is done, I assess and think how this time period should be filled with strength and blessings to become a better person. I believe everybody has seasons throughout the year, for a different purpose. The purpose can be as small as reading a chapter in a book every day to something as big as being a good brother to your little sister because Mom's job means working in the evenings. A season can be when you create a goal to accomplish something within a time period or in the midst of life's twists and turns, you are put into a role that leads to growth along the process.

The timing of a season can start and end at any time of the year, but I believe the most growth within children happens during the summer. Kids get to have a sense of freedom and experience life outside of school during summer break. Not taking away from the growth of knowledge that occurs within school, but summer break will give life lessons that can't be taught in a classroom: the ability to learn something new away from school, go to a new summer camp, make new friends, work and save money, for example. Every summer brings a new task at hand--which brings me to Summer Juice. I wrote Summer Juice during the summer of 2018, when I believe I had more "glo-up" (a nice transformation in one's appearance) than any summer in my life. That year, I began my first summer with an NFL team, I had just graduated from college, I changed my hairstyle to look more bold and grown, I received more money in my pocket to be able to buy what I wanted, and I learned what it truly meant to be a professional. The only difference is that this summer glo-up happened after finishing school. My approach to Summer Juice comes from my idea that the growth that happens during the summer break has more glo-up than during the school year. Transitioning from school into summer is like parole to kids, where the environment is different and kids have free time...Glad to be out of the classroom cells that can feel like jail with some teachers (not saying all classes are like that). With the shifts occurring, finding one's self and identity in the midst of change is important, and I believe that the summer gives children idle time to figure it out.

A lot can take place within a summer that is underestimated in society. A kid can gain new interests, develop new habits and confidence that can help them have a better school year. Summer Juice shows how the glo-up is not just about the change in looks, but a change in state of mind. Leveling up, so to speak. When a kid comes back to school the first day after the break, you will know that they're a new person after reading this book.

Diving into Summer Juice, it is a neighborhood tale following the glo-up process of the protagonist named Josh, a kid who is shy but has personality locked inside that tends to open when he reaches comfortability in a situation. The more situations he becomes a part of, the better his confidence is while seeking his purpose for the summer besides his neighborhood job of cutting grass. It takes the constant words from his brother, his neighborhood crush, Charmin, and the neighborhood to remind him that he can do a lot of things this summer...It just takes work.

Summer Juice presents the glo-up process of Josh, but shows how the process does not happen overnight. The glo-up flourishes through hard work and development in little steps. It's about the process of working hard to accomplish goals, which unveils a change within a person that is not noticed until after the accomplishment. Not only does it take work, but it takes determination.

A lot of kids want things, but when the road to getting it becomes tough, they lose determination. Summer Juice presents determination in a perspective that pushes children out of their comfort zone, which I feel is lost today. The ability to seek was more present back in the day because kids didn't have much technology to occupy idle time. To have an adventurous summer required getting out of the house. Now that times have changed, I want Summer Juice to present the endless possibilities of adventure that can take place for a kid once they put the phone down. Kids have a lot of power during the summer break, but it takes determination to tap into it. Outside influences can also affect tapping into the power, which Josh relies on to stay moving forward.

The "juice" itself is what has influence within the story. Power and respect is what "juice" means in cultural terms, but it implies true colors for Josh and his peers to show a drastic side of themselves unconsciously, which makes the story interesting when situations occur. It has contemplation as being a good thing, while also being a bad thing due to the assumptions of how the seller makes it. The juice plays a role as the central figure of the story. It becomes the fuel to keep the determination to pursue purpose, as well as a reality check of what is present and what needs to happen moving forward.

Josh has his physical friends, but the neighborhood becomes his symbolic friend. It introduces itself through elements of a tough background that is hard to relate to at first meeting, but it grows on Josh how beautiful the personality of the neighborhood is, from the scenery to the people. Josh's circle is key, as for most kids in the summer, because the weather in the season for kids can go in a positive direction or in a negative direction. Summer Juice will show some instances of both, making your summer adventurous with this read.

First Encounters

Closed mouths don't get fed, but we sure get thirsty. Think about it. That piece of fruit is not going to find any entrance if my lips are tightly shut, but that juice will find its way to seep through the smirky ends. The same smirky ends that curl up when I see her jogging in the neighborhood. Just look at her, as I stop my lawn mower to admire her elegance. The first girl I've ever seen to float on concrete, with each stride so graceful. Then there is her face, so pretty and relaxed with no ounce of sweat, looking straight forward with no interest in me from her peripheral. But wait a minute. I do see her head turning toward my direction. The closer she jogs, the harder I stare. The harder I stare, the closer she jogs, squinching her eyes to get a better look at me. I may not be as noticeable as her hot pink crop-top, but I have a little presence that stands out. Our eyes lock for a small second with no expression from her face or interruption in her pace. Then, she looks at her Fitbit watch and returns her face forward on her jog.

The funny thing is, I didn't know she liked to jog for real until a month ago. I've been known to be a homebody; that is, until my older brother, Charles, came home from his four-year stint in the military. Since then, he gets me out of the house by taking me on joyrides, trying new restaurants, and showing me different spots in the city. He even got me to start cutting grass in the neighborhood so I can have money to go on little escapades here and there. Every time we pull out of the driveway before our rides, there she is...quenching my thirst as she jogs by. She doesn't go to the same school as me, but my brother is cool with her older sister, so he knew we were around the same age.

"One day you need to go say wassup to her," my brother always says.

I know I will, one day--when the juice is right. Right now, I'm still watered down with an okay taste, but once I enhance my natural flavor, I will be ready to drink this summer. Especially after a long jog on a hot day.

That reminds me. I don't know why I chose to cut grass today, wiping the oily sweat from my face. It's 100 degrees outside. All the grass and pollen are causing me to itch, and mosquitos have a sweet tooth for me this morning. Bouncing back and forth off my skin, craving a taste of me. Honestly, I don't know why I cut grass at all. I'm content with staying in the room this summer. You are never too old to watch occasional Boomerang cartoons all day. Boo'd up to the bed comforter while the A/C makes it hard to lift a muscle. In between cartoons are occasional looks on Instagram and daydreams about going on summer vacations. Summer parties too, where I pretend I have boys who want to take me to a party. The right guys who can help me rehearse the right lines to say when I find the confidence to talk to some girls, to where it works and one of them calls me the next day when I get their number. But noooooooo...I'm out here pushing my life away. Every little step I take with the lawn mower, I hear the bed calling my name and a possible cry out from the sweet tea in the fridge, too. My mouth is getting watery as I think about it. Let me hurry up with this job before I melt and drain into the sewer.

"Here you go." He puts the money in my hand and closes the door. I look at my hand and I see $10. $10?!!! I swore I told him $20. Plus, his yard is like a football field. Man, I swear my neighborhood is cheap as hell. Acting like I'm one of these Mexicans who will do more for less. I would say something, but that's too much energy and he looks like a football player, sooooooooooooooo that's dead.

Like Moses, this walk back home is about to feel like 40 years. Walking from one side of the neighborhood to the other side in hopes of reaching the Promised Land. The motivation of the sweet tea keeps me walking, but the little nutrients of no breakfast pulls my head down. The heat is unbearable, too, where eventually, my breath shortens, my shoulders fatigue, and my legs begin to cramp in the process. The drip from the water hose across the street looks so good as I push by. "Drip drop. Drip drop" as I listen to the splash that comes from the outside faucet. I feel like a dog ready to run over and get me a sip. But suddenly, over the hill, I see a big sign shining bright, like the Gates of Heaven are opening. "Sonny's Lemonade" is what it reads. I don't know Sonny, but I heard about him in the neighborhood. Sonny is Frank Lucas to the hood. . . or he was your average weed dealer, until the feds did a sweep over his campaign. After the punishments, he resorted to little hustles to make money the clean way, turning over a new leaf-and now I'm about to walk to his next hustle.

"Sir, I don't know if you need lemonade or some milk," Sonny laughs.

I just look at him and shake my head, yearning for a cup of lemonade. The weird thing is that I don't see any signs of lemonade on the table.

"Where's the lemonade?" I ask.

"Oh, it's right here," he answers as he reaches down to take it out of the cooler behind the stand.

Sonny puts it on the table and looks at me. "Nice and cold for ya."

The cold air sizzles off the bottle. But I don't remember lemonade being green last time I checked. Plus, there are some green flakes in there.

"Why is the lemonade green?" I ask.

With a little smirk and snicker, he says, "It's the green tea mixed in, with tons of mint leaves."

I know there must be more ingredients that make the lemonade green. "What else is in it?" I ask, scratching my head.

Sonny smiles and mentions, "Lemons, special sugar, and a dash of Hawaiian Punch."

"Can I try a sample?" I need to make sure Sonny isn't lying to me.

Sonny replies, smacking his teeth, "Does it look like I got sample cups? Trust me! All my customers love my drink, especially on hot days like today. Not to mention, you'll feel like a new man afterwards. Plus, rejuvenated, especially on a hot day like today. Also, sir, you look parched and dry. From ya walk, from ya talk, and probably ya game with the ladies."

I pretend to laugh with him and quickly switch back to a straight face.

"Look, just buy a drink for $3 and you will feel better on your way back," says Sonny.

I stare at the drink, contemplating about buying it. My mind was already set on the sweet tea in the fridge and this drink looks too exotic, probably spiked. Everything about the situation is telling me no, but I barely have saliva to swallow, so I convince myself yes.

"Okay, fine," I say. I open the bottle and drink every ounce of it. Surprised, I look at Sonny with a satisfied face. "Mmmmmmmmm!"

"I told you," Sonny replies.

I pay him and start to leave, feeling my taste buds two-stepping on my tongue for joy as I walk away. The taste is tropical, and I know it has something to do with the green color. "All I needed was some green eggs and ham and I would have been good," I am thinking, and laugh to myself.

Five minutes into walking, my heart starts pounding a little faster, with my veins throbbing to pop out my skin. My eyes widen, the hairs on the back of my neck stand up, and my chest pokes out like I did a chest pump. Suddenly, music raids my ears when there is nobody outside playing music, synchronizing my head to bop and my body to jig uncontrollably. Next, my mind taps into an exciting, yet complacent frenzy. All nerves and senses are not in my control as if somebody is remote controlling me. Cars drive by and beep their horns, or they roll down their window and say, "Ayyyyyyy!" Neighbors in their yards look at me and laugh, but I don't care. Right now, I'm the "life of the party" as I push my lawn mower. A flash mob by myself. I feel like a new man, ready to attack the world. Nothing can seem to ruin my vibe. Then I hear a large bark down the street.

My heart instantly drops with bass, despite how my body is under this trance. Next thing you know, there is a full-grown Great Dane, with his mouth open, running a 40-yard dash toward me. I see the dog while I am dancing, and then my adrenaline rush kicks in, turning my trance off. So I take off full sprint, looking for the nearest car. I thought my speed increased with the adrenaline boost, but it stays the same speed that got me in last place during the 100-yd dash in Field Day a couple years ago. The dog runs me down quickly, snipping my Achilles in the back.

"Awwwwh," I yell and fall abruptly. The dog begins munching up my shirt to where it begins to tear. First, it's a punch. Next, it's a kick, but the dog keeps coming for me. So, during the scuffle, I begin to think that I have to hit the dog with a combo move and a haymaker. All of a sudden, I think about when I was playing my cousin in a game of Tekken on PlayStation 2. I had this one dude named Marshall Law. He was a crazy martial arts character that was great at getting out of gang ups. Every time my cousin's character jumped me, I would get Marshall to throw a 2-piece punch combo with an explosive kick to throw him in the air and land on the ground.

The combo moves strike me as my executive move to execute along with my haymaker kick to land and connect. As I keep stiff-arming the dog, I begin to load my fist and my kick leg at the same time for the right amount of power. My last stiff arm pushes him off balance, giving me time to set up punches and put myself in position. My fists tighten, and my arms begin to coil. The dog comes toward me, and here we go. My first punch lands him in the jaw and the second punch lands him in the eye, causing him to fall back and bark a shrieking sound. After he recovers and comes back to attack, my leg boots up and my foot kicks the dog in the throat, flying the dog in the air like a saucer.

When he lands, I yell, "Bitchhhhhh!" The dog lays on the ground, shaking and moaning. I stand up and my body goes back to my flash mob trance, except I am happy to have my body under the trance this time. With a big smile on my face, I feel so proud, bouncing on my toes like I won the heavyweight fight. Dreaming that a girl would come and say, "You go, boy." The funny thing is, I look ahead and see my jogging crush heading my way. I'm smiling and feeling myself, thinking she's coming to see me. It's only right for her to make this moment special. She smiles a little, as she is catching her breath while maintaining her stride. Abruptly, her face changes, with her eyes getting big and her mouth getting wide.

"Missy!!" she yells with a painful tone. She begins to sprint toward me, but not for me.

Instead, she begins to check the dog's pulse and inspect more on his body. Certain areas that should move create shrieking sounds from the dog. It's like watching a concerned nurse and a fallen soldier. After checking the dog, she quickly glances at me with a furious look.

"Did you do this?" she asks. I just stand there, bouncing on my toes, smiling uncontrollably; I can't stop it. The more she sees my lack of care, the more she becomes enraged.

"Yeah, I did it," I announced with full joy over the situation, continuously bopping to my own beat. She walks a little closer and smiles at me. Admiring my groove as her eyes traces my shoulder jigs.

Fwapppp! She lands a big slap to my face and walks back to her dog. My cheek starts tingling, along with my face, but not in a good way.

"Owwww! Why'd you do that?!" I shout.

"What do you mean?! Look at my dog!" she snarls back. "You need to be glad I didn't call Animal Services on you."

The dog lies there, helpless, fuming all my crush's gas on me. I feel bad, although I feel like a different "me" in this situation. The tingling trance begins to melt and ooze out a new, confident color. A color that has never been a part of my color scheme. When a girl puts me down, I usually take the "L" and keep it moving. Now, my heart has an inner determination to seek her forgiveness, which was abnormal to me.

"Woah, woah, woah! Please calm down, baby," I say.

"Baby?! You don't know me!" she exclaims. The funny thing is that I dreamed about me calling her baby one day, but not today.

"I'm sorry, I'm sorry, I'm sorry. What's your name?"

She gives me a mean look as she continues to evaluate Missy. "Charmin," she says in a nasty tone.

"Ooo nice; like the toilet paper?" I reply.

Charmin's face begins to turn red. "No! Like my mother's name is Charmaine, and then she came with Charmin. I swear I hate people who say that," she yells while taking out her phone and dialing like she is about to make a call.

Instantly, I think about Animal Services, so I grab her phone with no permission and say, "Wait! Can I start over? Pleasssssssse?"

She rolls her eyes and crosses her arms with frustration, looking at her Fitbit. I can't believe what I just did. I'm surprised at myself.

Looking at Charmin face to face almost throws my confidence out the window. Man, her face is beautiful.

"Look! This is not what you think. Not too long ago, I was pushing my lawn mower down the street. Then, your dog came out of nowhere and chased me."

"Why did you run? Missy doesn't bite," Charmin replies.

"Oh no. Trust me. She was coming for the kill. With her eyes wide and her teeth out and her Aaaa.... Aaaa.... Chooo!!!!" I sneeze over Missy's face while I am talking...and Charmin is hot!

"Ewww!! Look what you did!" she screams.

"I'm sorry, I'm sorry. Please--"

"Boy, ain't no more please!" Charmin cuts me off sharply. "What you sayin' is not true and I'm not going to stand here and act like I believe you. Goodbye."

I feel bad, but I still stand with pride and dignity. Charmin does another check-up on Missy as I reflect on my mishap. Missy's body is still for a long time, but then her head starts moving. Her body perks up, her tail begins to wag, it looks like she is back to normal as she springs to her feet. Suddenly, Missy looks at me and a growl follows.

"Wooooof!!!"

The bark sounds like Missy calling me out of my name. After she insults me, Missy runs over and attacks me again.

"Awwwh!" I yell, thinking Missy is going to bite me with her head engulfed in my stomach. Thank God she doesn't, but Charmin swiftly dashes to the rescue and pulls Missy off of me. First, she yanks her off of me and pulls her to the ground. Next, she spanks Missy to the point where I can see that she has a little crazy side... that I oddly like.

"Now sit, or else!" Charmin threatens. She walks over to me and apologizes. "I'm sorry for that. You were right. Missy has never done that." I try to get up like a tough guy, but I have to hold my stomach on the way up. "Oh no, are you okay?" Charmin asks.

"I think Missy bit me," I say, with fake hissing effects.

Charmin walks over in a comforting way and says, "My house is five houses down the street. We can fix you up there. It's the least I can do. Once again, I'm so sorry."

"It's okay. It's okay," I say, getting up slowly for the effect. I agree to go with her, but I have never lied so hard in my life. A small fib has never hurt anybody. Little does she know, the reason why I'm grabbing my stomach is because I have to use the restroom.

Charmin, Missy, and I begin walking together as I push my lawn mower leisurely. She wants to walk fast, but she notices my slow pace due to the Oscar-winning sore gestures I display. As long as she believes my stomach is the main issue, I can tough out the other problems. At the same time, slow movement equals slow conversation.

"How long have you had Missy?" I ask.

"Since I was little," she answers.

"You never thought about a small dog?" I counter back.

"No," Charmin says in disagreement. "What is a small dog gonna do if somebody was going to try me? The big dogs are the intimidating factor. Plus, they are so cuuuute."

Her response baffles me. "Who would dare try you?! The way you spanked Missy changed my outlook on you."

Charmin looks at me, perplexed with my statement. "What do you mean (your outlook)?"

"Well, I honestly thought pretty girls like you weren't the type to fight."

Charmin gives a facial expression like she is about to drop some knowledge.

"First of all, I'm not pretty. I'm beautiful," she says. "Secondly, I don't fight, but I know how to defend myself. Lastly, you should be thanking God that this girl came and saved you because Missy would've chewed you up."

I reply, "I would thank him for that, but now I'm thanking him that she's taking me back to fix me up."

I smile and look at her, but then, she hits me with a gross face and responds, "Don't thank me too hard. It's only for a moment."

"A lot can change in one moment," I say on the sly.

Charmin has a weird look on her face, and doesn't say another word for the rest of the walk to her house. Meanwhile, I'm smiling in my head, high-fiving my conscious, thinking, My "spit game" rehearsals are definitely keeping me alive.

She lives in the only red brick house on the street. It's hard to miss it.

"Where can I put my lawn mower?" I ask.

"You can put it next to the garage door," she responds.

I place it next to a bush where it's less conspicuous. Charmin opens the door for me to walk in, and a cherry aroma instantly hits my face. One inhale and exhale welcomes me in her lovely home. Her house is captivating with its red interior. The family took the cherry red color theme and ran with it. The living room is draped with red silk and linen, too. If they would have bought some red lights, their whole display of cherry red would have been complete. Missy walks in and barks. Out of the kitchen door, it looks like Charmin's older sister comes out to meet us.

"Missy! Where have you been?" she asks.

Missy wobbles over to her, looking to be loved. But she slaps Missy hard in the face.

"If you leave one more time, I'm taking you to the dumpster!" She quickly grabs Missy by the ear and throws her in the dog cage. Watching what just took place helps me to learn two things run strong in her family: their beautiful genes and an aggressive slap hand.

"Sorry about all that. Hey, how ya--Woah! What happened to you?" Charmin's sister is startled by my scratchy scrappy appearance.

"Missy attacked him multiple times," Charmin tells her.

"Really?! Look, I'm so sorry. We've got a First-Aid kit in the back," her sister offers.

"She even bit him in the stomach," Charmin says.

Her sister's face tenses up. "Are you serious? Let me see." She moves closer, ready to peek at my wounds.

"Ummm, can I use y'all restroom first?" I interject.

"Sure, it's down the hall to the left."

•••••••••••••••••••••••••••••••••••

I walk to the restroom with urgency and shut the door. My stomach has a bubbly feeling and I know I have to piss the feeling out. Hopping up and down, I hurry to unbuckle my pants and then I go.

A sigh of relief comes out of my mouth. As I'm peeing, I notice how my urine is steamy as it splashes in the toilet. In addition, it's green, like lemonade. It puzzles me, but I keep it movin' because I know they are wondering why I am taking so long. I flush the toilet and begin to wash my hands. During mid-wash, my body begins to shake like an earthquake. My ears pop, my chest sinks in, my jitteriness disappears, and the feeling of my inner, confident self depletes. My whole bodily experience ends with a fart so loud it could be heard outside the restroom.

"Nooo," I whisper, pacing back and forth in the restroom. My mojo is gone, and I lied about my stomach. No idea comes to mind, but I know I have to walk out before they wonder about me. I wipe my hands and walk out toward the living room, panicking about how I'm going to play this situation out.

"Everything all right in there?" Charmin's sister asks.

"Yeah."

"Okay then, go sit down on the couch. I'mma get the stuff and look at the bite."

All of a sudden, it just got hot. I'm so nervous that I tremble out, "Uhh okay." I walk over to sit by Charmin on the couch. I don't say a single word, until she cracks open a question.

"So you cut grass?"

"Yeah," I reply.

"This is a hot summer. Why do you do that?"

"To get money," I answer.

"Get money?" Charmin snickers.

"I mean make money," I say, frowning on my last response.

"Okay, cool," Charmin says, and then looks at me in a joking way. I feel like she is giving me a signal, but I don't know for sure. Her smirk said a lot with her one eyebrow up, one eyebrow down look. Not to mention, the eyebrows made her eyes glisten naturally as if I'm looking through a hazel prism. Like the cool guys do in movies, I decide to scoot a little closer to her, knee to knee, foot to foot... a sly entrance into her personal space.

Immediately, her eyebrows arch and Charmin shoves me off. "Boy! What are you doing?!" she shrieks. My face is clueless, and my tongue is tied.

"Uh, uh, uh, nothing."

Charmin is in such disbelief. She gives me a mean mug. "Charm, are you coming?" Charmin yells. So that's her name, I think to myself. Charm's feet echo down the hall.

"Here I come." She has a basket of first-aid supplies and a bag of ice. "Okay... What's your name?" she asks.

"Josh," I reply.

"Okay, my name is Charm. Nice to meet you," she says with a smile. "Lift your shirt up so I can see."

"Wait, for what?" I ask.

"Lift your shirt up so I can see the wound!" Charm commands after my answer.

"Uh...uh...okay." My nerves begin to fly around this room as if a shotgun went off near a flock of crows. I am beginning to sweat. The pressure of my lie is building. I'm staring down at my shirt and playing with it, hoping another idea comes to mind.

"C'mon!!!" both Charmin and Charm yell, looking at each other in agreement.

"Okay, okay." I close my eyes and slowly lift my shirt dramatically. My heart pounds as I pray for anything to get me out of this situation.

Out of nowhere, a loud ringtone goes off.

Riing! Riing! Riing!

"Oh snap! That's my job calling. Handle him, Charmin," Charm commands, quickly leaving the room.

Charmin makes no movement as my brush-up encounter is still fresh on her mind.

"I can fix myself in the restroom if you like?" I say.

"Yeah, you do that," Charmin says, throwing shade.

I walk back to the restroom and think about everything that has taken place. Putting my hands to the sky, I'm relieved, yet disappointed by how I misguided her look. I shake my head to calm down, and then look in the mirror.

"This is the summer for somebody to know the 'new' me. .. why not her? Come on, Josh," I say out privately loud, as if I was a coach talking to his team before a game. After a nice pep talk to myself, I walk out of the restroom to the living room.

Charmin asks, "Is everything okay? You good?"

I reply politely, "I'm fine. Thank you."

"Anytime," she says, looking at the door. "Well, I got something to do, soooo, yeah. Glad I could help."

"Of course," I reply, shrieking inside because I don't want to take this "L." I walk toward the door and then stop and turn around.

Charmin makes a peculiar face and asks, "Did you leave something?"

I take a deep breath and exhale, turning around. "No, I wanted to ask you something."

"Wassup?" she asks.

I start off in a timid manner. "Well, every time I go to hang out with my brother, I see you jogging. Every day. Why is that?"

Charmin stands there with no movement and has a blank face. The first time her guard looks like it's about to come down. She sits down on the couch and rocks back and forth.

"What's wrong?" I ask, as I walk to sit by her on the couch.

"Nothing, nothing. I just thought about something." Her tone is emotional, as if she is about to cry. I didn't mean to strike a nerve.

"C'mon now. You helped me, and now I want to try to help at least," I say.

Charmin takes a deep breath and begins to talk. "Well, for the longest, from a little kid to earlier last year, I was extremely fat. Almost close to obesity. Little kids would tease me, and girls would talk about me. My sister and my family were talked about as well. Plus, my dad was the same way, too, but his condition was horrible. So bad that he died this past January."

"Oh no. I'm so sorry," I say, thinking about that experience and how that would have been.

"No, you're fine. I just started reminiscing out of nowhere, but I'm fine. From that situation, it motivated me to start jogging every day and stay healthy."

Charmin telling me her story gives me so much respect for her, but it's making me feel bad for myself. "Wow, that's amazing. If only I had that same motivation in my life," I say.

"What do you mean? You cut grass in 100-degree weather," she says as if she can not understand why I think this way.

"Not because I want to," I counter.

"Yeah, but for money," she adds.

"I don't even care about the money. My brother got me to do this," I say.

Charmin has a peculiar look on her face and asks, "Who doesn't care about money?!"

"Me. It's not like it's going to make me happier," I say with irritation.

"True, but it can create you an opportunity toward happiness!" Charmin says as she matches my tone.

I smack my teeth in frustration. "No, it won't!"

"Why not?!" Charmin asks.

"Because the money is just going to stay in the house all day!" A heart-wrenching nerve erupts. "It ain't like the money got friends. It ain't like the money got a car. It ain't like it got moves on the weekend. It's not like the money even has confidence to tell his crush how he feels. The money doesn't have nothing!!!" I explode, gasping for air as I try to calm down. I can't believe that just came out. I'm winded, I'm sweaty, and the left side of my chest hurts suddenly. Meanwhile, Charmin stares at me, confused, wondering what just happened.

"You okay?" she asks.

"I'm okay," I say, overwhelmed.

Neither of us speak for a minute. I'm staring outside the window. Charmin stares at the ground. Then she looks at me. The same look she gave me when she dropped knowledge on our walk here.

"You might be right. That money doesn't have the car, friends, the girls, or anything . . . but it still has value. Honestly, there is nothing wrong with staying in the house, especially if you are adding value to yourself, but it sounds like you don't do none of that right now?"

I look at her with disappointment and then look away with guilt.

"So stick with cutting that grass. It's adding value to you whether you like it or not. Plus, it's the summer! You need to get outside the house. Don't let the A/C keep you in your feelings all summer. Let that summer breeze and the smell of grass motivate you to switch all that up. Then, by the end of the summer, all that value will increase your self-worth. More worth than a car, more worth that will give you new friends, and more worth for your crush to notice."

Charmin surprises me as she finishes on a high note. It's inspiring to hear this motivation, especially from my crush. I will not forget how she says "this will attract" her, as I'm plotting ideas in my head for later.

"You're right," I said. "Hearing this will definitely make me want to do better this summer, especially if we both got something for motivation."

"Exactly. You better do better or we're gonna fight," Charmin laughs, switching up her sentimental tone.

"Hold on," I said. "I thought beautiful girls don't fight?"

Charmin chuckles and says, "You're right. My bad. I'm glad you remember."

"Of course. Beauty's hard to forget...well, I mean beautiful quotes," I say, not feeling smooth at all as I click my tongue in embarrassment. The delivery of that line is so bad, I declare a mandatory "spit game" rehearsal tonight in my head. Charmin holds herself from giggling and turns her face away from me. I believe she is smiling as I look carefully to see her face. To avoid this awkward moment, I look toward the window. Looking outside causes me to think about the time.

"What time is it?"

Charmin takes out her phone and reads out loud, "5 o'clock."

"Oh snap! I got to go. Me and my brother are supposed to leave for Centennial Park at 6."

"Ayyyyy! I go there all the time, especially to sit by the lake," says Charmin joyfully.

"Really?! Let me know next time you go," I say, rushing toward the door.

Charmin stops me in my tracks and asks, "Well, how am I going to let you know?"

Charmin smirks and stands there in silence, luring me to ask what I've always rehearsed since my first crush in elementary school. Timara Price, a pigtail cutie, who always had me stuck when she said something to me. Getting her number could have been a reach in second grade, but we could've walked each other to the bus after school. A couple playdates here and there. I never had the guts to shoot my shot then, but I feel that my shot is open today and she wants me to score.

"What's your number?" I say, trying hard to contain my blushing to where I cannot hide it as I grab her phone, but I stay strong. Doing my best to make it seem like getting girls' numbers is normal. A mild-mannered face with a stiff mouth showing stiff emotion. I play my "too cool for school" act until she watches me walk out of her house. Once I grab my lawn mower, I strut back to my house with joy and happiness, gassing myself up and rocking to an imaginary '90s R&B song that fits the occasion. A long walk, but I was too happy to feel the burden of its distance. Just in time, I make it to my house. 6 o'clock on the dot. As I walk in the kitchen for something to drink, my older brother, Charles, asks, "Where have you been? And why do you look beat up?"

"It's a long story," I say, rushing my way to the refrigerator to pour me a cup of juice.

"Okay, spill it to me."

After a voracious gulp from the tallest cup in the cabinet, my voice is refreshed to spill the tea. Well... I mean juice.

"So, after cutting grass, I do my best to come home, walking in quicksand on these streets until I run into Sonny."

"Oh, for real? What was he doin'?" Charles asks with the same peculiarity I had when I saw his sign.

"He was selling lemonade with this big table on the corner of the street. It was weird because the lemonade looked more green than yellow, but it tasted like heaven though. After I left him, I was almost back, until this dog chased and attacked me."

"Wait, what?! You okay?"

"Well, now I'm okay, thanks to Charmin, the girl that stays jogging in the neighborhood."

Charles grins. "Oh, really now?"

"Yeah. She took me back to her house and cleaned me up. Her and her sister were checking me in all my spots like we were in the ER. Too close sometimes."

"And you say this in a bad way?" Charles asks sarcastically, confused as to why I'm trippin'.

"Well, no. At least take me on a date first."

Charles busts out in laughter. "Boy, if you don't go somewhere with that. So was that it?"

"Well, sort of. I had a nice little convo with Charmin and then went about my way."

Intrigued by the terminology of "nice little convo," Charles reacts swiftly to ask, "Woah, woah. What do you mean a nice little convo? What y'all talked about?"

I don't roll my eyes, nor do my cheeks turn red, but I feel embarrassed to tell Charles about our conversation, because it went horribly wrong at first. Plus, we talked about some deep stuff, too. She gave me the talk that's more important than the birds and bees for any shy, closed dude.

"So we talked about basic stuff first. Then we talked about things like why she likes to jog and why I cut grass. Once that dried out, we said goodbye, and here I am."

Charles smacks his teeth in disappointment. "Man, there were no beans in that spill and you didn't get her number." I smile at his disappointment, avoiding his look because the excitement of getting her number is written all over my face.

"Stop playin' with me, Josh. Did you get it? Did you get it, Josh?!"

I do my best to stay stone cold, but my heart can not contain the joy. I've had a crush on her for a long time, and today was my day. "Yeah I got it."

"Let's go!" Charles comes and jumps on me, squeezing me like I made a Kobe buzzer-beater. He lets go abruptly like and then a lightbulb goes off in his head. "Wait, ask her to come to the park with us at 7. I'm going to bring her sister, Charm, with us too. I'm just glad to know that you don't have to third-wheel this time."

Chuckling with a coy grin on my face, I nod in agreement, taking out my phone. Having a number outside of Mom and Charles is an achievement for me. If Netflix and my pillow were people, their phone contacts would run all down my call log. I go to her number, ready to type, but then I freeze. How should I start this off? I think to myself.

"Uh, Charles? How should I start this off?"

Charles looks at me, dumbfounded by my question. "Josh, just say 'Let's go to Centennial at seven.' Don't ask, just tell her. Wait. You know what? Just give me your phone." He grabs my phone out of my hand.

"Wait, what are you doin'?" I ask, perturbed about what he is going to do. I walk on to him to see what he is doing on my phone, snooping to see that he is texting Charmin. Everything is fine until I see "Aye, girl" in the text.

"Woah, woah!" I say, yanking my phone back in a displeased way. "I don't talk like that." In the moment, my brain made an appointment to make sure Charles is present at my spit-game rehearsals next time.

Charles becomes irritated at me, checking the time all in the same process. "Look Josh! You have 30 minutes to make something happen. If not, you just won't come. I can't support you as a third wheel, knowing that you didn't do all you can to get her to come. Time is ticking, bro," he says to me and walks off. The pressure is on, but I just need the right words, the right verbiage, the right approach to make it easy for her to come, but how?

I look at my phone and it says 6:35. Oh snap, I need to move. I hurry up the stairs uncontrollably, taking off my clothes because I know that I'm not going to smell like outside when we're outside in the park. When we talk, she's going to smell lily flowers and my cool breeze body wash blowing through the air. I grab my towel and head to the bathroom. I turn the knob and it's locked.

"Open the door, Charles!" I say, banging on the door.

"Give me like 5 minutes!" Farting sounds let off. "Ooooh, make it 7!"

"C'mon man." I'm annoyed by his bowel's lack of urgency.

"Did you text her yet?!"

Hesitant in my answer, I say, "No, not yet!" I hear the toilet flush as his response, giving me an underlying feeling about how he feels about my response. The faucet turns on for him to wash his hands and then he opens the door, shaking his head with his funky aroma inviting me to come in.

Walking down the hallway, he turns around and says, "It's now or never," and then keeps walking.

I go into the bathroom, nauseated by his stench. I turn on the tub water and pull the handle for the shower. I take off my towel, grab my phone, and sit on the toilet to look at some videos. Inspiration needs me more than this shower as the steam from the hot water makes it feel like a sauna, adding more pressure to my life.

I search random websites for pickup lines. It was funny because I saw really good ones like "Are you free tonight or will it cost me?" to bad ones like "Did you fart? 'Cause you blew me away." Something I can see Charles using and he still goes out with the girl. Every pick-up line got worse as I scrolled, so I go on YouTube and search random videos for it.

I click on this one video where this one guy is saying pick-up lines from different states in the country. The video has me dyin' in the bathroom, especially after he does my state. "Aye shawdy, no cap I just want to know can I be your move for tonight?" The man on the video says it well, but I know I can say it better than him. I step in front of the mirror, wiping the moisture off so I can get my face right. Keeping my composure from laughing, I raise my one eyebrow to show the look that this ain't a game. Then pull my eyes down and have them stare sharp like a needle to freeze the mirror. Lick my lips and smirk to give that desirable appeal and lastly, clear my throat so the voice matches the alluring look of my face.

"Aye shawdy, no cap I just want to know..." In mid-sentence, the door quickly opens and Charles walks in, as I'm naked in my cool man pose, shocked with no expression on his face. I quickly grab my towel and take defense.

"Damn. We don't knock anymore?" I say with frustration.

Charles grins and then busts out laughing, teasing me in my birthday suit. "Bro, what are you doing?"

"I'm just going over my pick-up line to ask Charmin."

Charles giggles some more and catches his wind, wiping the tears out of his eyes for stability. "Man, you just textin' her to come along with us. This is not do or die," he says, grabbing his brush off the sink. "You got 10 minutes, Josh." Charles closes the door in amusement.

Oh, snap, I think. I jump into the shower and scrub-a-dub-dub all around my body, squeezing all the body wash lotion out the bottle. Suds flyin' and bubbles floatin' everywhere. A car wash in my own bathroom. I turn off the water and jet down the hallway to my room, catching the wind to help speed up the drying process. Wiping myself off, I snatch out my good T-shirt. Looking nice and crisp like the dry cleaners pressed it. Then I see my torn shirt from today on the ground. Sad and disappointed as I pick it up. I throw it in the trash as a mature decision. The old me would have patched and sewn it up. Post-shower sweat is still apparent, but I don't care. I throw on my underwear, my shorts, and my shirt. Looking for my phone with only 5 minutes to spare, I go to her contact and text "Come to the park with me at 6." No "please," no question mark with no time, so I click Send and throw my phone over the bed because I don't want to think about it. My heart races in my body before I can race downstairs, sweating out the body wash before she can smell it. Waiting for the notification, Charles yells, "Let's go, Josh," before I can hear the answer I need to hear. I grab my phone and come downstairs, having trouble breathing when I face my brother.

"Sooo?" Charles asks.

I look at my phone and there is no message in sight. I check the message board to see if she sees it and what do you know, the message didn't send.

"Noooooo!" My heart jumps off the cliff of my lungs. I can't believe it. Charles comes closer to see my disappointment and shakes his head.

In the midst of my loss, Charles' phone rings off. Briing! Briing! Briiing!

Charles picks it up and puts it on speakerphone.

"Y'all on the way?" Charm asks in concern.

"Y'all?!" I hear. "What do she mean by y'all?"

Wait a minute. I look at Charles in amazement.

Charles gives me a sly smile and says, "Yeah, we comin'. Just 'bout to get in the car right now." "Okay, don't have us waiting."

"Us?" I hear again, looking at Charles.

Charles laughs and says, "All right," and hangs up the phone. "Let's go, bro." He rubs my head like a poor little dog. Like a father to his son except I don't like when he tries to father me. Sort of wish he could've had a little faith in me. Could I have blown the situation out of proportion? Probably so, but it doesn't matter because the long day I had does not come to an end yet.

Job Loss

"Damn, everybody is at the park today," says Charles, making his third lap around the parking lot for a spot.

"There's one right there," Charmin says, pointing to the lone space in the corner. Charles accelerates to the parking spot in a hurry and backs in like an old man, or like a guy from what he heard. Checking the mirrors all the time with the little vision he has . Josh struggles to get out of the car due to the little room left with Charles' seat leaned back. Charmin and Charm come out of the car, breathing in the ambiance that is Centennial Park. Kids playing ultimate frisbee to the left. Shirtless joggers with their dogs on the right. A green, serene wonderland where nature and humans can call a truce and chill, while keeping the place clean. The day is bright with a pinch of sun in the sky to create a relaxing scene going into night time. The four walk from the parking lot to the main playground, where little kids are running wild and free. The pace of their walk is easygoing until Charles comes to a smooth stop.

"Okay, guys. Me and Charm are going to hang over by the swings over there. Where y'all going to be?"

Charmin says, "We gonna' go by the lake and chill over there."

"Okay bet. Text me if y'all move somewhere else or on y'all way back," says Charles. "Oh yeah. Make sure this one behaves," he says, inferring his statement to Josh in a sarcastic way. Josh fakes a laugh and walks away with Charmin, shaking his head.

Charm and Charles walk over to the swing set, jaywalking through the traffic that is the kids playing.

"Not it!"

No, no, no, you're it! Bam!" a little kid says, running into Charles' knee.

"Gahhh damn!" Charles yells in pain, hobbling while grabbing his knee. The little kid falls down and gets back up with no pain, impervious to what life throws at him.

"Aye, little man, watch where you're goin," Charles commands.

"Sorry," the little kid says with a buoyant smile and runs away.

"You okay?" Charm asks in concern.

"Yeah, I'm good," says Charles, exhaling in heavy intervals while walking to the swings. Charles and Charm get on their swings and drift slowly. Charm chuckles and says, "You better be good. Besides, things probably hurt more over in the army."

Charles shrugs her comments off his shoulders and begins to swing with more speed.

"So how does it feel to finally be home?" Charm asks, getting ready to swing herself.

"Well... I don't know," says Charles, looking off in the distant sky. An orange flame cloud guiding the sun to its sunset.

"What you mean you don't know?! You're back home from overseas, you're healthy, you have a job."

Charles sharply interjects, "Man, forget that job. I don't know how people love desk jobs, anyway," he says with salt.

"Why you don't like your job?" Charm asks in confusion.

"It's boring there. I have to wear dingy suits. I'm the only black person there. The co-workers there are uppity. Sitting at the desk filing papers puts me to sleep even when I drink all the coffee in the world."

"Man, you better stop sleepin' on the job or you gonna get fired," says Charm, swinging higher into the air, matching Charles' velocity.

Charles laughs. "Honestly, I would not care if that happened."

Charm rejects as she swings to his level, coming close to touching the sky. She answers and says, "All right now. You gonna end up like your broke little brother, cutting grass for a living."

Charles hears Charm's words and catapults off of the swing into the wind. Soaring like an eagle until gravity humbles him down to the ground with a soft landing. He turns around, looking at Charm, and says, "Chill out. Besides, my brother is working hard to earn an honest buck."

"I'm sorry. I'm sorry...I see his grind," Charm apologizes. "It doesn't go unnoticed. Trust and believe. But if he is thinkin' bout doing something with my sister, he's gonna have to come with a little more than just a measly money-making job," says Charm with frankness.

Charles shows a weird look as if her comments have a stench to it and says, "What you mean?!"

Charm searches for the words to say, set back by the tone of Charles. "Well, my sister is outgoing and likes to be adventurous and see places. Go out to eat and talk deeply about the world. Your brother? He's boring, too shy, and stays inside all the time. From the times we talked, you always say how he is lazy too."

"See, I told you these things, but that was from me not being there all the time, but now I'm home for a while and I'm gonna get him right. He got juice, it's just that somebody has to open him up, and I believe Charmin and I are the right ones to do it."

"Nuh uh. Why it has to be my sister?" Charm asks.

"Because unlike you, she actually likes somebody in my family."

"Oh, here we go again with this. Nobody wants to talk about that right now. The point is, he needs to come with a little bit more if he has a shot with my sister," says Charm, rolling her eyes.

"Pscht. Girl, whatever," says Charles.

With a candle light of sun in the corner of the horizon sky, parents grab their kids and leave the playground. The sound of kids playing is no longer present, but the only sound that remains is the shrieking of the swings.

"So tell me this. How you think life would be if you were here permanently?" Charmin asks.

"Honestly, it would be great," says Charles, giving Charm a coy grin. "I can pursue painting seriously, I can stay close to my brother, I can stay close to you. . . . I can see it all one day."

Charm lets his answer settle, spurring a silence in the breeze, and then nods her head in agreement, grinning at Charles. Charles grins back in unison.

Charm begins to notice how dark it has gotten with the little light that is near them.

"Let's go see what they doin' by the lake; besides, you got to be right for work tomorrow."

"Okay," says Charles, getting up from the swing.

●••••••••••••••••••••●••••••••••••••••••●

Next morning, the cell phone goes off in vaudeville fashion. The beginning melodies of Al Jarreau's "Mornin'" blazes into Charles' room, taking a couple minutes to reach the inside alarm clock of Charles. A heavy sigh rings off after a few minutes and Charles begins to move a little to wake up. In the meantime, Al Jarreau continues to break it down with his soulful voice.

Mornin' Mr. Radio, Mornin' little Cheerios

Mornin' sister Oriole

Did I tell you everything is fine...in my mind

(Snooze)

Charles slithers back his hand after pressing snooze into his covers. Breathing heavily, he goes back to his dream. Once he gets ready to fall asleep for his ten-minute slumber, his phone goes off in reckless fashion, ringing up a storm with the thunderous vibrations.

Briing! Briing! Briiing!

Charles pulls his cover off of his body and reaches for the phone to pick up. He wipes his eyes softly, snorts snot out of his nose and whispers, "Why hello?"

"Good morning, Charlie boy! You sound fresh like my coffee."

Charles clears his throat to wake up his tone. "Why not yet, but I will, John. What seems to be goin' on?"

"So the company has a potential employee and would love for you to show him around," says John.

"Me! Why me?! I just got there three weeks ago," says Charles in confusion.

"Bossman wants you. Plus, you should know more about the company now, so why not?"

Charles hesitates in disappointment. "Well, I guess."

John is ecstatic. "Great, Charlie boy! Come to work at nine and we'll see you soon."

Charles sharply interjects with a not so well tone.

"Woah, woah, woah! At nine?! I usually come to work at ten."

John laughs in a hysterical way and says, "Whatever Bossman says is whatever goes, so I'll see ya soon. Ciao." John hangs up the phone, leaving Charles pissed on the other side.

Charles opens up his blinds to refresh with some sunlight through the room. The rays glaring through the blinds show it's a beautiful morning. Nice and warm for a day of work. Charles moseys over to his closet to pull out his shirt and slacks and then lays them on the bed. With no pep in his step, Charles stays in his grouchy funk. He irons his shirt first, sliding and pressing the wrinkles for a crisp shirt. Co-workers do call out wrinkles as a joke in the office, which Charles does not like. Moving to the bathroom, a quick shower takes place. Charles normally sings to help clean his pores, but the radio of his voice is not on. Charles breezes through the morning routine in a lackadaisical way, but with some pace because 9 am is quickly approaching. Walking into the kitchen, he checks to see what to eat for breakfast in the cabinet. His breakfast of champions starter kit includes strawberry Pop Tarts, a cup of fruit, and orange juice. Charles pulls out the Pop Tart box, finding that it is empty, and smacks his teeth in disappointment. He goes into the refrigerator for juice and fruit, but there is none left either. Wondering what happened to the food, Charles stares blankly into space, seeing a vision of Josh drinking all the juice and eating the last Pop Tart before going out to cut the grass this morning. 8:30 on the dot, Charles snaps out of his vision and walks out to get in his car. It's only been two minutes and Charles is sweating through his shirt. The heat is well and alive for any victim that comes outside. Once Charles turns on the car, he quickly lets the A/C blast to cool every heat particle that is left in the car. He backs out of the driveway and drives off, rollin' down the street sipping on nothing but ice cold air. Refreshing as it feels, it does nothing to satisfy his thirst until he drives upon a big sign on the corner of the street. "Sonny's Lemonade?" he says, driving slowly due to the stop sign. Sonny walks to the window of Charles' car in a cheerful mood. Charles rolls down his window while looking at his phone clock.

"Damn it's cold in there. I wish I had that cool breeze out here," says Sonny, feeling refreshed from the breeze.

"I feel ya on that," Charles says kindly.

"Now is it me or do you look parched?" Sonny says, squinching his eyes. "Look, I know it's the morning time and it's early, but it seems like you could use a nice, refreshing drink." Charles says nothing, but thinks about the truth in his words, contemplating if he should buy one.

"Look, bro, I know you have to go to work, but please believe this lemonade will help energize you for work. With that shirt and tie on, it looks like you work in a building full of …" Sonny looks left, then right, then bends closer to the window and whispers, "White people. Am I right?"

Charles nods his head in agreement.

"So what do you say? It's a nice cup of lemonade with your name on it. Sizzlin' too."

Charles agrees. "That's fine bro. Let's make this quick before I'm late." Charles pulls up closer to the stand, waiting for his cup. Sonny runs to his cooler behind the stand and runs back with the ice cold cup and says, "That will be $3."

Charles looks at the drink and is disturbed by the green-colored elixir, mistaking it for something that tastes disgusting rather than something delicious. "Wait a minute, bro. What is this?" says Charles in bewilderment. "Last time I checked, lemonade is yellow."

"Well, it's the green tea mixed in with tons of mint leaves that makes it that color," Sonny says, smiling.

Charles looks at his phone and loses all suspicion, digging quickly in his wallet to pay him. "Okay, look, here's your $3. If I get sick off of this, it's ya ass."

"No problem. Before you go, taste it," Sonny encourages.

Charles inspects around the cup slowly. He brings his nose around the top to smell it and then looks at Sonny.

"Go ahead." Sonny nods.

Charles brings his mouth to the cup and sips carefully, dissecting the taste off his taste buds and gums. Smacking his lips for the last, minor detail. A drink critic with a last sincere backwash and swallow. Then he looks at Sonny in amazement and says, "Damn, this shit tastes good! What you put in here?"

"See, I would tell you, but don't you have to go to work?"

Charles shouts in reaction, "Shit!" and drives off, screeching tires and everything. Ten minutes away, Charles drives his usual route, feeding pressure to himself because he encounters four red lights in between the highways and byways. Sitting at 8:55 with five minutes to go, he drives through a yellow light on the nick of the switch from yellow to red light. With the destination in his front mirror view, he sees the building's entrance. One more street to pass and he's on time. Charles continues to cruise until he sees an orange sign that says "Detour."

"Wait, what?" he says to himself, shocked. He follows the arrow to go around the building to get inside through the other entrance. Charles turns right and follows the road to success. The final destination does not lead to tardiness. Just a few more blocks and he's safe. To be on time is on time until railroad lights begin flashing, with the white gate arms coming down. Who thinks to put a railroad by an office building in the first place?

"No, no no, noooo!" says Charles, slamming his steering wheel in anger. He's pissed, snarling at the fact of being late. 9 o'clock strikes as the time. Taking his loss, he decides to remain composed. Being mad does no good, so Charles sits in frustrated peace. He takes a look down the railroad track to see if the end of the train will show, but it does not. Ten minutes later, it still doesn't show. Dripping with sweat down his fused face ready to spark, he decides to finish the cup of Sonny's lemonade, gulping every lick of drop. Charles takes a look to find the end of the train one more time, seeing the same result, and loses his gasket. "Damnnnn!" Charles yells, jumping in his seat in tantrum-like behavior. The steam that comes out the teapot is hot in Charles, whistling harder than ever until Charles' body turns off the stove. The A/C feels so much colder than before. Air puffs blow out of his ears like the steam blower on the train. Charles' eyes circle around his sockets and bounce from left to right in a pinball machine way, landing slowly back together with his eyelids hanging low. The heartbeat that is racing from the disappointment of being late slows down. Somewhat attentive, yet nonchalant and aloof. Every beep in his brain is a slow heart monitor, where every thought comes at a time.

Beeeeeeeeeeeeeeeeeep!!!

"Huh?" Charles slowly looks up and sees that the train is gone. Then, he slowly looks back to see the line of cars behind him. Driving off on his sweet time, he makes it to his job and parks. Sauntering to the elevator, he runs into his co-worker, Dana.

"Good morning, Charles."

Charles rolls his neck over her direction slowly. "Waaaaaaaaaaazzzzup girl." He grins at her in a delirious way.

Dana looks at Charles in a shaken way. "Are you okay?"

"Neva betta baaaaaaaabyyyyyyyy. Neva betta," he says, bumping into her uncontrollably after the elevator shakes to the exact floor. Dana catches him in his fall with his head all into her chest.

"Myyyyyyyybad girl, myyyyybad." Laughing in a joking way, he lifts himself up.

"I'll see you later," Dana says, walking off the elevator in a hurry. Charles walks off and strolls into the company office. Before, it was a matter of life and death. The bar to make it to the building was set pretty high for Charles, but now it is low. Pretty low for him as he tightropes into the office.

"Charlie!!!" John screams, pacing over to him in an upset way. He adjusts his tie and collar, maintaining the perfection in his attire. "Why are you late and why does your shirt have wrinkles?"

Charles laughs in a hysterical way, snickering, "Seeeeeeeeeeeeeee I don't know." He shrugs his arms with a large smile on his face.

John grabs Charles by the shoulder tightly and begins walking to Bossman's office, his eyes narrowed in on Charles's face like a missile ready to fire if willing. "Look I don't know what is wrong with you, but we need this guy, so you need to get your head on straight. Capeesh?"

Charles giggles past John's seriousness and says, "Capeeeeeeeeeeeeeeeeeeeeeeeeeesh!"

"Bossman, here he is." John brings him to the head office.

"Hey, Charlie. I want you to meet Maxwell, a potential employee for us. All we need for you to do is show him around and bring him back for our office lunch day. Okay?"

"Okayyyyy Okayyyyy, Bossman," says Charles, chuckling. He salutes Bossman and quickly grabs Maxwell's hand and takes him outside the office. Bossman is perplexed by his answer and demeanor, looking at John. "Maybe that's what they do," he says, shrugging his shoulders.

"Um, what is your name again?" Maxwell says. Charles hangs his arm around Maxwell and says "Charrrrrrrrrles."

Maxwell pinches his nose after catching contact off Charles's breath. "Riiiiiight. Quick question: Are you inebriated?"

"Bwahahahahahahahaha! Silly Maxwell. Noooooooo! That's stuuuuuuuuupid."

Charles escorts Maxwell to the back of the office space and starts his tour from there.

"So welcome to F.H.N. Consulting Agency, also known as. . ." Charles takes a look left and a look right, moves closer to Maxwell, and whispers, "Finally Hiring Niggas agency. Bwahahahahaha! You feel me?" Maxwell is at standstill, confused at the likes of Charles. They begin to stroll past some cubicles in a gracious manner. "This is Maddy. She does the, does the, does the . . ." He peeks over her cubicle to see her name tag. "Ohhhhhh yeahhhhh. Strahhhhhtegic Communications."

"Oh my God! Charlie!" Maddy says. Charles turns around softly. "What I doooooooooo?"

"All the wrinkles on your shirt!"

Charles look at his shirt and chuckles some more. "Myyyyyybaaaad." Maddy makes a strange look at him.

Walking past Maddy, Charles takes him over to John's office.

"This here is Joooooooohn's office. He's our Senior Viiiiiiiiiiice Prezzzident." He squeezes Maxwell's shoulder hard to emphasize the point. "Hey, John! I'm awake nooooooooooooow!"

Looking at Charles, he softly laughs. "About time, Charlie boy! You know I'm always woke." He raises his fist to the sky.

Maxwell looks at John and then looks at Charles in a peculiar way. Charles tries to contain his laughter, but it pours out as he walks away from his office. The two take a tour of all three levels of the building, strolling past the Technology Department to the Financial Consulting Department and meeting the public affairs team to the janitorial team. Charles shows him the agency boardroom to the first floor break room. Consecutively on all trips, Charles is a goofball ready to reckon with. His tie falls out of his collar and visible sweat stains come out of his armpits. Shirt wrinkles that the janitorial team mentions, but it is time.

"Alriiiiiiiiiiight Maxie. Let's go upstairs to the agency luuuuuuuunnnnnch."

They take the elevator to the 3rd floor and walk to the luncheon held in Bossman's office. There is a plethora of food and co-workers are standing on both sides of the office. Charles begins to take a plate until Bossman grabs him by the side and tells him to come here.

"Hey, Charlie, does Maxwell seem to like it here?"

"Loooooooooooves it here, Bossman," says Charles, leaning toward him.

Bossman smiles. "That's good because the agency needs you gentlemen to keep things woke around here, you know what I mean?"

Charles looks at him in a misconfigured way. "What do youuuuuuuu mean, sir?" He taps his foot rapidly.

"Give me a second, Charlie. I'll tell you after I make this toast." Bossman lifts his cup, saying, "Hello everybody! Excuse me!" The crowd of workers stops talking and looks over to him.

"I hope everybody is enjoying this delicious food thanks to my friend Isaac from Gorm's Catering. Here at F.H.N, we do these types of lunches every month to connect and come together over a nice meal. Day by day, we provide our services to help companies maximize their potential. Slaving over our computers, operating off of multiple cups of coffee, falling asleep over the phone. . ." Charles hobbles during mid-speech, bouncing on his toes and tightening his crotch for relief. Knowing that he can't sit down, he leans on the side of the food table. The table gradually tilts forward, but Charles doesn't feel it. After slowly tilting past the holding point, the table falls forward, causing the food and Charles to fall in dismay. The drops of the food and the slam of the table causes commotion, directing the attention of the workers toward him. Bossman stops in mid-speech in an irritating way and yells, "Dammit, Charlie! Why are you PEOPLE so clumsy?!"

Charles hears those words and sits up after falling. There's an angry look on his face where the Bossman's words are detected, releasing a lever in his mind to go off. "Maaaaaaaaaaaaaaan, what you mean "you people"?!!"

Bossman snaps back, "People like you. Can never sit still. Always moving and causing noise."

Charles picks himself up and kicks the pans of food at the people and all around the office in anger, causing Bossman to be appalled. His mouth opens wide in great dismay and steam comes out of his head. "Charlie, boy! You are FIRED!"

Charles looks at Bossman in a demonic way and says, "Goooooood! Because I don't want to work for people like youuuuuuuuu!"

He storms out of the office in disruption, barging into the restroom. Quickly unzipping his pants, he pees into the urinal. During his piss break, his stomach flips and turns. His eyes somersault back and forth, back and forth. The last bit of his pee is steaming and his ears pop for confirmation, oozing all the drowsy sensation out of his body. He flushes the urinal and walks to the mirror, looking at himself in a puzzled way. Touching his eyes and feeling his cheekbones, he evaluates himself and what just happened. After washing his hands, he walks back into Bossman's office, catching austere looks on the way. Bossman looks at him in surprise with a tormented demeanor.

"Look sir. Please, I apologize for everything that just happened, but please don't fire me. I need this job," says Charles.

"It's too late, Charlie. You already made your desecration and there is no turning back now. Besides, Maxwell will take your place. Now, leave the premises or I will call security."

Charles walks out of the building and into the parking lot with a grey cloud over his head, sorrowful about what just happened. He drives home with less obstacles than he had this morning. When he pulls into his driveway and parks, he reaches for his work bag and notices a green smudge on the bottom of his lemonade cup. Looking at the smudge with his peculiar eyes, he feels a sense of suspicion with the drink, but he lets it be, grabbing the cup to throw it away. Walking into his house, he falls into bed and takes a nap, wrestling in his sleep of thoughts over today's events. His unrestful sleep lasts 'til the evening sun glares through his blinds. He wakes up with a groggy face, yawning in a helpless way. Charles changes out of his slacks and his "wrinkled" shirt, throwing them on the floor for the hamper to get them later. Then he grabs his phone and crawls back in bed to call Charm. Four rings go and then she picks up.

"Wassup?"

"Where you at?"

"I'm at my house, why?"

"Can you come over? I need to talk," Charles says with grief.

"What's wrong? You okay?"

"Yeah, I'm cool. I just need to talk."

Charm says, "Okay. Gimme five minutes."

Charles says okay and hangs up, grabbing his robe. Walking downstairs, he runs into Josh, who is making a hefty sandwich. Josh sees Charles's demeanor and asks, "You okay, bro?"

Charles saunters past him like a zombie, nodding his head, and moseys into the basement. He tiptoes through the landfill of junk that takes up space in the basement. Once he sees his canvas stand, he stares at it. No color of illustration except the white, blank slab. He takes a few deep breaths and walks over to his art collection next to it. The works of greats such as Aaron Douglas, Jacob Lawrence, Ernie Barnes, and a couple of his own pieces that he accumulated over the years. As he is looking through his collection, he hears a couple creaks as if someone is coming downstairs. Charles looks over and sees a clumsy silhouette coming downstairs.

"Man, y'all need to do something with all this," Charm says, walking through the piles.

Charles looks at her and stretches out his hand to help her

through the mess. He takes all their stuff sitting on the dusty old futon and places it somewhere else for them to sit.

"So what's up?"

Charles wipes his head, exhaling heavily. "I got fired today."

"Wait, what?! What happened?!"

"It's crazy to where I don't know where to begin. It was a weird day because I felt out of whack the whole time. All I know is that I accidentally spilled a rack of food at the company luncheon during my boss's speech."

Charm smacks her teeth and chuckles. "Damn, Charles, and you say I'm clumsy?"

"I know, I know. But for real. Tell me why after I make a mess, he gets mad and yells, "Why are you people so clumsy?""

"You people?!" Charm exclaims. "Ah hell naw. Forget that job. Rather be unemployed than work for a racist company."

"I feel you, but I don't know. I need this money."

Charm looks at Charles with authority. Her eyes ready to get a grip on him. "Look! Forget the money. You gotta have dignity at the end of the day."

"Yeah, but I need to do something, Charm," says Charles. "Or this may be a short summer."

Charm looks at the canvas first and around the basement, connecting the dots for a way to solve his problem. Then, it hits her after she slaps a clutter fly by her nose.

"I know what you can do."

"What?" Charles says with wonder.

"In the meantime, do like a yard sale and sell all this junk to get by. I mean look at all this. I be forgettin' this is all your stuff. A whole time capsule in one basement. Plus, you can sell your own art and some from the art collection over there."

"Girl, I am not going to sell my art collection. These are limited editions. Vintage stamps." He walks over to blow the dust off some of his pieces. "Plus, nobody ain't gonna want to buy my art," says Charles, rejecting her suggestion.

"Stop sleepin' on yourself. These are great paintings and you never know who in the world might like them. Plus, you need the money."

Charles looks at his art and then looks back at Charm with intrigue, rubbing his chin to think.

"So then how would we get the neighborhood to come through?"

Charm smiles. "Leave that up to me and Charmin."

Charles walks back to sit on the futon, and then looks at Charm in acceptance.

"Let's do it."

The Yard Sale

Another day, another measly $10 after I tell people twenty. Maybe my voice comes out as "twenty" and they hear "ten." Last time I checked my Southern accent isn't too strong and when I talk to Charles, he hears me. One day, these people are going to hear me correctly and hear me well. Walking back to the house with the lawn mower doesn't feel too bad anymore because I know I can catch Charmin jogging and she knows who I am. If I see something bright pink or neon in front of me, I might just jog to it. If I smell some apple fragrance out of the blue, my Charmin senses will be tingling, sniffing a trail to see where she's at like her dog, Missy. Look at those sprinklers over on the lawn, shooting up and down. It reminds me of the sprinklers in the lake at Centennial where me and Charmin were chillin'. Sunset in the sky. Fireflies all around us like mood lanterns. Don't let me tell her that because as much as she likes being outside, she hates bugs. During mid-conversation, I told her it's a ladybug on her shirt. She flipped and almost had a heart attack when I showed her. Not even caring if it means good luck. I guess I'll know that next time.

Speaking of next time, I need to think of more things to say. Spit-game rehearsals are cool, but now I've graduated to the level of conversing. The way she was talking made me realize I need to say something more or eventually, she won't say anything at all. It was sort of hard too, because hearing her talk is invigorating. So much "I'm gonna," so much "I want to" when she speaks as if she dreams about it at night and tells the world about it in the daytime. She told me she was gonna bring me to the neighborhood clubhouse, where she helps look after little kids in the neighborhood. A sort of summer camp, you can say. They bring smiles to her face, she says. She says she wants to do something big for them this summer. She doesn't know what, but she knows she wants to do it. Whatever it is, I know I'll be down.

Almost to the house. Just a few more houses down.

My phone begins to vibrate in mid-walk, tingling the right side of my leg. It's been a while since I received a call, I wonder who it is.

Oh snap. It's Charmin. I clear my throat, grunting my "do re mi fa so la ti do" vocal chords until the pitch of my voice is perfect.

"Um, hello?" I say like a smooth operator.

"Hey, it's Charmin."

"Hey, wassup?"

"Come to my house ASAP! We got some things to do."

"What things to do?!" I say in an excited but nervous way.

"See, you askin' too much. I'll explain later," she says.

"Okay. Well, can I go change first?" I look at the sweat and the filth of outside in my attire.

"Naww, just wait real quick."

"Uhhhh okay." And then she hangs up.

I wonder what the mission is. It must be a big deal if she is fine with this funky aroma turning her red house lawn-cut green. (sniff, sniff) Oh Lord, I smell horrible as I lift up my shirt. I guess I'm not getting a hug tonight. Well, let me wipe the sweat off my face so I can look more presentable.

"Ding-dong! Ding-dong!" I ring the doorbell, swatting the gnats in the process.

The door opens and it's Charm, happy to let me in with a squinching face.

"Oh my God. Why didn't you change before you came over here?" Charm says with disgust.

"She told me to come over ASAP, so I guess here I am," feeling like Johnny on the spot.

Charm takes me to Charmin's room. When I walk in, I see a palace filled with Hello Kitty paraphernalia and Beyonce posters. Destiny Child's Beyonce to Lemonade Beyonce dancing off the walls. A Hello Kitty bed set that looks soft, it could put me to sleep. Meanwhile, Charmin is locked in on her laptop by her bed, with no wave or hello as I walk in. She doesn't feel my presence until I tap her on the shoulder. All I can see on the screen is the making of a flyer.

"Oh, hey! Ewwww," Charmin says, grabbing her nose. "Yeah, I should've had you change first, but it's all good I guess." She looks me up and down.

I prepare to take a seat on her bed, but then she stops me in my tracks before I can lay a muscle, telling me to sit in her room chair rather than her bed and making me feel like a peasant.

"So look, I don't know if you heard, but Charles is planning to have a yard sale this Saturday and it's our job to spread the word."

A yard sale? "What exactly is a yard sale?" I ask.

"It's when you gather everything old or antique from your house and sell it in your front yard for the neighborhood to see. Sort of like a flea market." There's perplexion on my face as I still don't understand her.

"What's a flea market?" I ask.

"Damn, Charles!" she says in frustration. "Basically, what we're doing is selling all y'all stuff outside your house for the neighborhood to come see, look around, and buy."

The terms she told me are something I have never heard. I honestly didn't know we could sell in front of our house. Picture us selling things, bringing more people into our little cul de sac. Sounds like a complaint ready to take place; although this sounds like a great idea since Charles got fired, but the question is is my stuff being sold with his? I don't believe I have much junk downstairs, but I do need to check before he sells away something that is dear to me.

"So I guess what you want me to do?"

"Well, I'm 'bout to print out a bunch of flyers for us to go hand out tomorrow morning."

"Tomorrow?!" I say with confused conviction.

Charmin laughs and busts into sing-a-long. "Tomorrow! Tomorrow! I love you, Tomorrow!"

Calming down to think about tomorrow makes me realize tomorrow is not a hectic day. It's just the fact of doing it in the morning, interfering with my summer morning cartoons.

"What time in the morning?"

"How about 9 o'clock?" Charmin suggests.

"Do we have to do 9 o' clock? That's usually what time I wake up."

"Hmmmmm, okay. What about 9 o' one?" Charmins says jokingly. Funny as it sounds to her, it's not as funny to me.

"Look, that is the best time where people in the neighborhood are up out of bed, cooking breakfast, getting ready to do yard work, so 9 o'clock is a good time, trust me," Charmin says with wisdom. The way she explained it seems like she has this down to a science. Locked in on her computer configuring the day and right time for us to go. A formula more complex than algebra. She's the teacher and I guess I'm the student, so all I can say is okay.

She passes me a couple poster boards with markers and glitter.

"Don't make these posters basic. Put some pizzazz on the posters and make it pop for people to see miles away."

Laying the posters on the floor, I tap into my inner artist. Thinking about the times I would look at Charles when he would paint and draw. I needed a vision. I needed some flavor, but I also had to think about what is a nice sign that will help turn even the speediest car around to come to the yard sale. Let me see.

First things first is the glue, thinking I need something sticky to put glitter on the board. The glitter is the sprinkles on top, so I guess I'm working backwards in this case. I scribble glue streams along the edges of the poster, taking me back to arts and craft in kindergarten. I get in sticky situations on accident, making a mess with the glue as it sticks to my fingers and then sticks to my shirt. Charmin, from time to time, looks over with a smirk to see me in my process, wondering how my creative process will come to light.

Glitter is next on my list, seasoning the poster like I'm cooking. Charmin looks over and sees my glitter handiwork, saying, "Don't put all that glitter on my floor." I hear her, but I dabble a little more glitter on the poster, just not as excessive with my wrist. Little sprinkling with the fingers.

Then I begin to draw blocky letters. Nice and large for the average eye to see as if it were a billboard. "YARD SALE" written with nice penmanship for a boy; plus the blue marker outline is neat. Lastly, I take the markers and color in the letters. Coloring outside the lines hasn't been my thing, but I'm making sure it doesn't happen as much. Blue and yellow markers will capture the neighborhood's attention. Yellow makes the sign bright for the eye while blue makes the words bold to read. I look at the poster like museum art, seeing if there is anything else to add or do. Charmin looks over to see my masterpiece, recognizing the Picasso in my poster.

"Look at you and your creative self," says Charmin, grabbing my poster and stapling a flyer to it.

"Okay, is there anything else you want me to do?" I say.

Charmin looks around the room for confirmation and says, "No, you're fine. Just meet me at my house in the morning and we can start."

"Okay," I say, walking over to give her the poster and anticipate a goodbye hug, arms wide open while walking to her. After she grabs it, Charmin looks at me with my ready-to-hug posture and stance. She grabs her nose, chuckling and sticks her arm out for a truce handshake. "Yeah, I just took a shower; maybe next time, kid."

A slight rejection, but I understand. I walk out of her house and push my lawn mower back to my house. A different walk because the street lights are on. Not as bad as walking in the sun, but not as safe either. The neighborhood is an oasis in the day, but it can turn into summer madness even on a regular night.

•••••••••••••••••••••••••••••••

"Oh snap!" I say, rising up Taylor Swiftly from what feels like a 22-hour sleep. I reach over to my phone and I see four missed phone calls from Charmin. Hopping out of bed with a quickness, I put on some clothes in fast time. Racing over to the bathroom, I splash water on my face, washing my face with one cloth in my hand and brushing my teeth with another hand. Multi-tasking and hand-eye coordination at its finest. Next, I wipe my face, grab my shoes, and run downstairs to grab my apple a day and run out. A dog running out the screen door. Where is Charmin? I think, walking down both directions of the street like Where's Waldo? A maze runner or a maze walker on some occasions. I call Charmin before I make my next move, but her phone is dead. Playing I Spy, I check every house, every door. Every front yard, every backyard. Every window too, if the blinds are open. Luckily, nobody called the police on me for trespassing. Over to the next street in the neighborhood and still no Charmin in sight. At least the weather is not too hot, so my energy is up and my sanity is clear. The one thing in sight is the lawn not cut on the next street. If I had my lawn mower, my business could have been booming today. Wait a minute, is that her? A bright neon glow from afar, stagnant at the doorstep of the nicest two-story on the street. A yellow wooden house with a lovely rooftop. The urge to run is turned off from all the walking, but maybe I can show her the pedometer on my phone, showing her how I searched high and low for her. Halfway there, I see her turning around from the yellow house.

"Charmin! Charmin! Charmin!" I yell, jumping up and down, waving my hand.

Charmin sees me and keeps walking slowly, as if I were a mime screaming her name. A ghost in the flesh. I trot to come a little closer and get to her before she goes to the next house.

"Charmin!" I yell again and she doesn't say anything again. I run to her, grabbing her shoulder, but she jolts her shoulder away from me. I walk by her to get her attention, but she continues to ignore me. Walking to the doormat, she knocks on the door and stands primly waiting for them. I can't believe she is ignoring me. A few breezes go by and nobody comes to the door.

"Charmin, can you talk to me?" I beg. Charmin ignores me a third time and walks off in hard silence, leaving me to myself. First time a girl ignores me and I can't believe that she's the first one to do so. I've never had this treatment before in life, but I don't think I can stand for it. I come in front to stand in her way, grabbing her slightly.

"Get out the way," she says with malice. I stand there in silence with a sorrowful look on my face.

"I can't believe you disrespected my instructions like that! You only had one job and you blew it."

"Look, I know!" I plead. "But please forgive me. My alarm didn't go off."

"Right, right. That's still no excuse. I knocked on a bunch of doors and spread the word, so honestly, you don't have to stay." Charmin says, walking off.

I know I messed up, but I will put in my contribution. I may have started off the day bad, but I can finish out strong. It's time for me to prove it.

I walk with her to the next house to the next house, where they have a front porch with a bloodhound patrolling the yard from his leash. Timid to walk over with her, I go anyway. It's just something about dogs in front yards that puts me on edge. It seems like if I put a smidge of anything on their lawn, their siren goes off to run to me and bark at me to death. Not to mention, the trauma of Missy is still fresh. Charmin keeps walking as if it's her yard, so I try to be brave for her, but the bloodhound mean mugs me to the doorstep, growling underneath his breath. Charmin knocks on the door and rings the doorbell. The front door window blinds open to where we can see the resident coming to open the door. The door knob begins to turn and the door swings open to this pristine white man, garmented in the finest silk robe with golden slippers. He looks at us with wonder and then Charmin speaks.

"Good morning, sir. May I first off say you look like a man with taste as I love your Gucci robe and attire. The silk fabric looks good on you."

"Why, thank you," the man says.

"I come to you today to let you know of a place where you can add more luxures to your household and your apparel. On Saturday, there will be a yard sale filled with antiques and things that will fit to your liking. Vintage Versace attire, golden accessories, a large inventory of fine jewelry. So to spread the good news, take this flyer. The address is a couple streets over and you will not be dissatisfied."

The man looks at her in an impressive way. "Necklaces too?"

"Necklaces, bracelets, rings, everything. Plus, some of them will be made of gold, silver, platinum, you name it. Just come early before others take them," says Charmin with hype.

The man accepts Charmin's words and nods in approval. "Okay, great. Thanks."

"Have a nice day!" she says and walks off.

I look at her and then look at myself, just wondering what yard sale she is talking about.

"What was that?" I say in confusion. "We don't have all those things you said."

"Look, the goal is to get all the horses to the river. They're gonna drink from the river. It's just that it may not be water," says Charmin, walking up to the house.

"Yeah, but what happens when they come to the river and nobody buys?" I say, scratching my head.

"People are going to buy something. Charm says y'all got so

much stuff down there that it's something for everybody. Everything will be fine."

Coming to the next doorstep, I sort of question Charmin's logic, but then again, she may be right. Charmin rings the doorbell a couple of times, knowing there are people here with three cars parked in the driveway. From the outside, I hear somebody walking downstairs and getting ready to open the door. This time, an older black man appears, grouchy in the face, but large ears ready to listen as he scratches his belly. He looks back a couple times due to something loud playing on television.

"What you chil'ren want?" he says.

"Good morning, sir! How you doin'?" Charmin says in a country twang.

"I'm doin' good. Can't complain at all."

"That's good to hear. We don't want to waste your precious time, but we wanted to let'cha know that there will be a yard sale goin' on this weekend a few streets yonder."

In the midst of Charmin talking, I look at her and wonder why she is switching up the way she talks to this man. Some of the pollen must have clogged her throat and it's easier to talk that way I assume.

"Well, I would love to come, but I got hoodwinked last time I went to a yard sale."

"Oh no! By whom? And where?" Charmin asks.

"Well, on the other side of the subdivision, I believe a long time ago. They sold me an electric drill that looked all fine and dandy until the drill never turned on when I took it home," the man said.

"Oh, I'm so sorry to hear that. Most yard sales are like Sanford & Son rink-a-dink swap meets that con people out of their money, but trust and believe we would not put you in that position. Ain't that right, Josh?" Charmin finishes, looking at me for words. Her pass of the torch throws me way off because I was not done learning from her.

"Uh, uh, uh, yes, sir! I mean yes, ma'am," I say, grinning at her and the man for backup.

"So as a young lady, I want to give you an honorary woman-to-man promise that this will not be like your last experience and you will find something that you would like." Charmin reaches out her hand for him to shake. The man looks at her hand, staring her dead in her eyes. An old Western faceoff with their sharp-shooter eyes drawn to each other as they shake hands.

"Okay. Do you promise the same thing too, young buck?" The man looks at me.

"Yes, sir!" I say, bringing forth my hand in a slow manner. The fact of knowing that we may not have what he needs gets to me, but I remain firm in composure for Charmin. He shakes my hand and Charmin gives him a flyer and he assures us that he will come. He closes the door and we walk off his yard with Charmin giving me a sideways demeanor.

"What's up with you?" Charmin says.

"What you mean?"

"'Uh uh, yes, sir.'" She repeats what I said. "Talk to the man. Talk to these people!" she says.

"Okay. It's just hard."

"What's hard about it?" she says.

"I mean it's just that I don't talk to grownups like that."

"You talk to your mom and dad, right?"

"Yeah, but I know them. I don't know these people." I guess Charmin's parents never told her "don't talk to strangers" as a kid because I follow that rule all the time. Most of my life, other kids and other adults had to say something to me before I would say something back.

"True, but you have to come to these doors with a little plan and present it to 'em like their house is yours or you're gonna give them a reason to slam the door in your face. Besides, they're really like big kids. Just look different."

Charmin and I walk to our next house that has a beautiful front yard filled with beautiful flowers surrounding the walkway. Red flowers to yellow flowers. Short plants to tall plants. Next to the door looks like a big Venus flytrap ready to eat us if we move one more step.

"Look, I'mma talk the majority, but I will use you for clarity for backup and support. Got it?" Charmin says, giving me the plan before she knocks on the door. Let me loosen up and clear my throat so I can play my role.

"Oh my God, she got jasmine flowers too?!" Charmin says with excitement, walking through her extravagant garden to see. "I love these." She kneels down to smell them. Seeing her so fascinated with flowers is interesting. I've always heard flowers are one way to a girl's heart, but I didn't think that was a modern thing to do. Maybe back in my grandparents' day, but I guess I'm secretly taking notes right now for the future.

"Awwwhhhhhhhhhhh!!" Charmin screams. Startling me as I see what happened as she cradles up on the ground with both hands on her face, bawling. I help her up with both hands covering her face, wondering what's wrong.

"What happened, Charmin, what happened?!"

Charmin removes her hands from her face slowly and what reveals is a bottom swollen lip. "Woww," I say, thinking she must have got stuck with something.

The house door opens and this lady walks out to see the commotion. A skinny little white lady with a sunflower dress and tattoos all over her arms. The kind of lady who can be in a rock band concert on Saturday and be sitting in church on Sunday. Pacing over our way, she runs to check on Charmin.

"Jesus Christ! What did you do?" She comforts Charmin while looking at her face. "Oooooo you must've got stung by a garden bee. Do you know what happened?" she says, looking at me like a suspect.

"Ummmm I don't know." There's a dramatic pause as she looks at me with displeasure.

"What you mean you don't know?! You expect me to come outside my house and see two kids in my garden. One kid is fine. The other kid is in pain and expects me to believe everything is neutral? First of all why were y'all in my garden anyway?"

Busted like a crook, ready to just get cuffed and take that miserable ride to the slammer, all I know is that I am helpless and innocent, breathing heavy in the moment. Charmin hears no answer from me and looks at me with anger and tears.

"Talk!" she yells with a lisp in frustration.

"So ummmmm, we were here to tell you about this sale." I grab Charmin's flyer and give it to her. She looks at it for a second and back at me in a questionable way.

"Okay, let me get her some ice and then we can talk," says the lady, walking Charmin and me inside her house. Walking inside, it's big and she has Greek statues and paintings over her walls and floors. The top of the stairs is a cathedral. A museum inside her house. Very regal like a palace. She takes us to her kitchen, where she has a lot of greenery and scenery. Fresh fruit on the table. Green plants around the counter and on top of the refrigerator. The kitchen has a different scent, organic and natural. Almost the smell of a farmers' market. Charmin sits down and looks at me in a disturbed way as we wait for the lady to bring the ice.

"Talk to her or I'mma bust your lip too," she whispers her threat.

"Okay, okay," I say in fear. My nerves are already shaking from her getting stung and now I have to explain to the lady. The lady comes back with a wet cloth full of ice, a leaf, and a towel. I clear my throat and try to relax as she directs her attention toward me.

"What is your name, ma'am?" I start off.

"My name is Victoria, but you can call me Vickie. What is your name?" She grabs Charmin to the sink and gets a leaf and some tweezers, scoping out her wound.

"My name is Josh and her name is Charmin."

"Nice to meet y'all. Well, not in this way, of course. So what happened?"

As she grabs the tweezers to remove the stinger, I let her know.

"So we were walking into your yard, getting ready to come to your doorstep."

"Awhhhhhhh!!" Charmin yells as Vickie moves the tweezers around her lip.

"Relax your face, sweetie. I gotcha. Continue."

Startled by her yell, I start back talking, but timidly. "Your garden and flowers are amazing as we noticed, walking to your door."

Charmin hisses and yells again. "Ouuuuuuuuuuchhhh!!"

"There it is." Vickie says, showing her the small stinger in her lip. She then grabs a cloth and soap and lathers it in the sink until bubbly, cleaning her lips while Charmin does her best to hold back the pain. Blood is dripping from her mouth, but she is taking all the pain.

"So then Charmin sees some flowers that she likes and runs to check em' out before we knock on your door. And I guess while she was checking em' out, a bee must have stung her on the way."

Vickie finishes wiping her lip softly and tells her to put the ice wrapped with cloth on her face.

"What flowers was it?" Vickie says.

"I believe the small white ones out there."

Vickie laughs and says, "Ohhh you talkin' bout the jasmine flowers. Them flowers will lure you in with their smell just like any other bee to collect their food. You must have closed your eyes when you smelled them, huh?" she says, looking at Charmin. Charmin nods her head slowly.

"Okay, well I guess you will have your eyes open next time you kiss the flowers." She snickers a little to lighten the mood. "So what's this about a yard sale?"

"Ummmmmm." Charmin gets up from her seat and gives me a grim stare with the ice on her lip.

"Okay, okay!" I say out of terror. "So me and my family are having a yard sale a couple streets over. I believe, right?" I look over at Charmin, and she nods her head in agreement, rolling her eyes at the same time.

"We wanted to spread the word to you because we have a lot of stuff that you would love."

"Oh yeah? Like what?"

"Well, we have jewelry, electronics from old Apple accessories to Samsung gadgets, clothes, dresses. . ." Charmin points to the plants in a conspicuous way behind Vickie, hinting me ideas.

"Plants as well. Gardening tools, seeds."

"Oh y'all have that stuff?" she says, giggling.

It makes me laugh, and I loosen up a little, saying yes when she knows that it's a no.

"Okay maybe not that, but we do have paintings."

"What kind of paintings?" Vickie asks with curiosity.

"My brother is a painter and he has great pieces that I believe you would like; plus, he has other paintings from other artists in his collection. He's very passionate when it comes to that type of stuff."

"Hmmmmm, okay. I might have to see then. I appreciate you for telling me." Vickie looks at Charmin. "How you feeling, sweetie?"

Charmin removes the ice and says, "It hurts to touch my lip, but I'll be okay."

"Okay. Well, is there anything else y'all need?"

I shake my head no and so does Charmin. Walking out of her house, I take my time so I can cherish her decor and the smell one more time. One day I might need to come back to see this again. As she walks us out her door, I turn around out of a gut feeling. "So will you for sure come to the yard sale this Saturday?"

"Yes. You will see me there," she says with positivity.

Leaving Vickie's house, Charmin smiles with her ice held onto her face, looking at me. "See, was that so hard?"

"Yes," I say facetiously.

"Well, get used to it because we have the rest of the street to go and you are the spokesperson," says Charmin, chuckling a little. Looking back, Vickie was cool. Talking to people comes with practice, I can say. I guess Charmin will make sure I'll be articulate by the end of the day.

●••••••••••••••••••••●••••••••••••••●

We finish the rest of the street by early afternoon with one more house that Charmin has in mind.

"What house do you want to go to so bad?" I ask with little to no energy.

"Old Man Williams' house!"

"Who is that?"

Charmin slows down her walk as if the question gave her chills. She begins to spill her story, despite the pain of her stung lip. "So Old Man Williams is this Vietnam War veteran, who bought a house in the neighborhood back in the day when it was all white."

"So was he like the first black resident in the neighborhood?"

"Mm-hmm," sounding like she has on a muzzle. She comforts her cheek while she talks.

"You had people that were cool with him being in the neighborhood, but then you had some neighbors who didn't want him there, especially when he became a police officer and joined the Neighborhood Watch. So legend has it that forty years ago, he and his son were notorious for selling delicious lemonade every summer, showcasing it at the yearly neighborhood block party. Then one year, he sold it at the block party and it made all the residents at the party sick, which caused them to blame his juice. He pleaded to everybody that it wasn't him and that it was a trouble-maker kid who helped him make it. Guessing he must have contaminated the juice. Nobody believed him, but what's crazy is that the trouble-maker kid died that same night mysteriously and the parents blamed him and the juice, causing him to go to jail for fifteen years. The only reason why his house kept up is because his son became the head of the household until he drowned one summer, two years after he was released for good behavior. When Old Man Williams came back, he was ostracized by the neighborhood until white flight took its course and black families moved in."

"So why is he not involved in the neighborhood no more?" I ask.

"I heard because he became a grumpy, bitter old man who would cuss kids out from his porch. Once he became 85 years old, he never would come on his porch anymore, but if a kid did anything to vandalize his yard, the next day they were missing. No evidence leading toward him or nothing. I believe now he is glued to his house at 90 years old, but I heard he still keeps an eye on the neighborhood from the inside of his house."

A part of me is glad to see Old Man Williams and his house, but another part of me is scared something could happen to us if we take a wrong step on his yard. I know I don't want to be on a missing person poster. Charmin leads the way to his house, which is not too far from the clubhouse. Every house on this block looks brand new except for his house. Old in style, the house is beat up with a woodshed board as his door and owl-eye windows with blinds that flicker every minute. Not to mention, the wind chimes jingle when there is no wind. Debating if it's worth it, Charmin nudges me to walk to the door, with her right behind me. The presence of the house gives me an eerie feeling as if he knows we are here. Before I knock on the door, I sense a jingle from one of the blinds on the window. I knock on the door slowly--loud, but slowly. Nobody answers the door after I knock a couple times. Once my patience to wait is over, I get ready to leave his doorstep with quickness, but Charmin stays, yelling, "Where you goin'?! Where you goin'?! Ouuuuuuch!" and grabs her mouth. To save the trouble, she folds a flyer and slides it under the door and then leaves. I wait for her on the opposite side of his brown-picket fence, ready to leave from the gloom that surrounds his house.

Continuing towards my house, I think about how Charmin

stuck by my side the whole time, watching me talk to people every house and schooling me on the walks in between. I laugh as I think about how she gave me this one piece of advice about painting a picture through conversation. Basically, telling a story or giving a visual through words of what would happen if the house owner came to our yard sale. Charmin is telling me to fluff it up, add color to the story, build it up like I'm giving an Obama speech. Instead of Yes We Can, we want them to say Yes I'll Be There. The craziest moment of the day dealt with this one guy named Mr. Luther, who was acting big and bad in an awful way. Although meeting him would change the game for me. There was an instance where he kept going on and on about his antiques and piles of junk in his place and why it was better, but then I sort of cut him off in a rude way, saying, "Well, why don't you have a garage sale and go to everybody's house and tell them to come to it!"

The man looked at me in a bold way, stepped back by my remarks. I wanted to walk away, but I felt the firm presence of Charmin behind me, so I kept my place. Then he says, "Maybe I will. It will definitely be better than your yard sale."

Charmin was ready to chew him out with a swollen lip. I could've supported her by yelling at him, but I knew I had to not get discouraged. For some reason, I knew that's what he wanted us to do. With a big sigh of relief, I painted him the picture with palettes of him walking down to our stuff seeing antiques and fortunes worth more than money.

"Oh, if I walked to your yard sale, would it have an old Dell box computer? Would it have the Ipod classic? Would it have the first PlayStation with the Mario games?"

I named anything and everything retro, brushing it up with exquisite art and vinyl records that he could finally listen to. The Michael Jackson Thriller LP, Basquiat pieces, autographed baseball cards, etc. One side of the painting is the truth and the other side is lies, making me feel like a cheap car salesman. At the end, I capped it off by saying, "Oh, I don't think so, but ours will and if I were you, I should be there," standing with my feet glued to his doormat and a broad chest like a statue.

Intimidated by my real man presence and Charmin's stance behind me, Mr. Luther caved in and grabbed one of our flyers. He got my number to make sure I'd be there, but I gave him a fake number. Charmin thought I gave him my real number, making her even more proud of me when I said I didn't. She continued to give me pointers all day, but smiled more along the way.

We did two more houses to cap off the day and then taped the poster board underneath our street stop sign. I walk her back and she gives me a hug, sweaty n' all, and went inside. She gave me a hug, sweaty n' all, and went inside.

Smiling from ear to ear, I felt like today was a good day. When I walk in the house, I don't see Charles, but something tells me he's in the basement with the door cracked open with a hint of light. Making my way downstairs carefully, I see Charles sitting in the center of the basement, painting in front of the canvas. To see Charles painting overlooks how some of the junk and things we have are lined up against the wall in groups. The electronics are together with the kitchenware aligned next to it. The appliances are neatly stacked. What usually looks like a landfill underneath our house is now an organized mess. Charles looks peaceful in the center of it all.

I walk over to look at what he is working on and the first thing that comes to mind is the raining black lines all over his canvas. He normally paints like his favorite painter Peter Max. The robust love he has for experimenting with vibrant colors, yet this one does not look like the other paintings in his collection. The structure is freefall, as if he's putting all his post-fired mood on the canvas. Out of order and out of whack. Black lines just scribbled to the point past abstract over what looks like a white desk. He looks back to see me, hinting that I might be disturbing his session.

"This looks different, Charles," I say with hesitation, not knowing how he will take it.

"It does, but then it doesn't." He continues to paint, brushing soft strokes.

"What do you mean?" I look at him with confusion.

"So whoever looks at it is going to be thrown off by the black lines raining on the desk, but underneath the madness will be the answer to its inelegance."

"Okay," I say with indifference. "You gonna sell this?"

Charles scratches his chin, saying, "I might. Honestly, I don't know if somebody would like this. It's not like we got serious art collectors in the neighborhood," he adds.

In my head, he doesn't know what I know or seen what I seen, walking by houses today.

"I guess," I say.

"How was going by the houses today?"

"It was crazy, but it was fun," I say, laughing at the moments in my head.

"You was really talkin' to these people?" Charles asks with curiosity.

"At first I wasn't. Then Charmin got stung by a bee, so then I started spittin', jivin', puttin' people on game for this Saturday."

"She got stung by a bee?!" he asks.

"Yeah, bro, but this lady named Vickie helped us. She got the stinger out, cleaned her up, gave her an ice bag too. She said she will come to the yard sale too. I believe she may buy one of your art pieces," I say with utmost confidence.

"Why you say that?"

"She had nice art in her house and plus, she looks like she 'cultured.'"

Charles starts giggling and stops painting, struck by my humor. "Well, I guess we gonna have to see how 'cultured' she is."

"I know, bro, I know." I get ready to walk back upstairs.

"Yo, Josh!" Charles yells. I stop, coming back before hitting the stairs.

"I'm glad your summer is going well. You sound different than last year."

"Thanks, bro," I say with warmth. It feels good this summer with my big brother here. Without him, I don't know if the summer would be how it is right now.

●┄┄┄┄┄┄┄●┄┄┄┄┄┄┄●

"Heyyy!!" Charles yells, running to pile jump on top of me.

"Ahhhhhhh!" I yell. I twist and squirm to get out of his chokehold until I find my opening and reverse slam him on my bed. No one is going to win on my turf as I try to pin him down. Using my featherweight strength, he lifts me up and slams me into the bed, pile driving until I give up. I fight, I squirm, I claw. After a long fight with no escape, I tap the bed with my hand. He gets up with his arms in the air like he accomplished something. "If I would have went to the army, I would have won too," thinking to myself. I look at my phone and I see that it's seven in the morning.

"Bro, why we up so early?" I ask, yawning with a wide open mouth.

Charles jumps off the bed. "Whatchu' mean? We need to get the yard sale set up."

"But I told them to come at 9," I counter back.

"Well, we need to get set up before then, so let's go," he says with enthusiasm.

I sprawl out on the bed for a second, closing my eyes in a meditating way. Thinking about how much work it is going to be getting everything set up, I massage my head. "Get up!" I hear from the other side of the house and then that's when I hop up out of bed. Charles has been gloomy all week, but he sounds blissful today. Making breakfast downstairs for us to eat as I smell the kitchen aroma. Not the Saturday morning cereal and milk, but the take-ya-time pancakes and sausage with the orange juice on the side. He turns on the speaker box and plays his clean-up music playlist. All his oldies but goodies he would say. I go downstairs and begin to get everything in place after a balanced breakfast. I grab the two long placetables and get ready to carry them out. The garage opens after I press it, coming downstairs. When I walk outside, the sunlight greets me with a summer breeze as its handshake. A beautiful Saturday morning in my eyes. I carry the tables to the front of the driveway. Our driveway is flat and our walk from the front of the driveway to the basement feels like forever. Thank God we have this handle dolly to carry our big stuff to the front. Plus, Charm and Charmin come over, creating the assembly line that we need. The dolly slides from me to Charmin to Charm to Charles. Sometimes we switch places, making it comedy when Charmin tries to move big appliances with the dolly. In the end, Charles and I move the majority of the things while Charmin and Charm help set up the table, so the aesthetics look neat when people come by. We look at the clock and it is 9 o'clock on the dot. Now the wait begins. The anticipation makes me excited like Charles because we have quality antiques and stuff.

Thirty minutes go by and only a few of our neighbors come by to see what we have. It irritates me a tad bit because the demeanor of our neighbors look interested when they walk by and then they walk off in the same demeanor with nothing in their hands. No buy from no one. Charles sits in his chair patiently, but he stays happy.

A whole 90 minutes goes by and nobody else shows up. It's weird because due to the logic of Charmin, homeowners are up, doing something that requires getting out of the house. Tapping his leg, Charles sits impatiently with his enthusiasm in deflation. Charm comes next to him every now and then to keep him lifted, but it does little to cheer him up. Charmin paces in circles, feeling iffy about the situation. She goes back to the garage and then walks over to me.

"Josh, come with me to the front of the street, so we can get cars to come our way." Charmin says, holding the poster boards and markers.

"Ummmm okay, but what about Charles and Charm?"

"They can hold it down by themselves," she says as I look back on them from the driveway.

We walk to the front of the street with a mission, hearing cars drive by, honking with nobody turning into our street. Coming closer to the end, we see Sonny's Lemonade Sign all surrounded by the stop sign. Squinching harder, we don't even see our sign underneath the stop sign.

What happened to our stop sign?! I say to myself.

Charmin sees all that I am seeing and becomes pissed, walking over with fire in her eyes. Sonny sees us, walks over and begins to smile at our presence.

"With all that walking hard, sweetie, you might need something to drink to cool you off."

"Man, I don't want your lemonade. Where is the sign we had posted underneath the stop sign?!" Charmin asks.

"Sign? What sign?" Sonny says, chuckling.

"Hmmm, I don't know. The sign where your sign is placed and located with the stop sign!"

"Honestly, baby.. ."

Charmin cuts him off with malice. "Nigga, don't call me baby!" She stares at his soul, ready to snatch him.

"Look, I'm sorry. Let's start over. My name is Sonny. Clean Sonny, who came over this morning with no sign underneath the stop sign and decided to post here for the lemonade stand. I don't know if you heard, but I've been selling lemonade all over the neighborhood."

Charmin comes closer to him over the stand, yelling at him. "That's a lie! I went jogging this morning and the yard sale sign was still underneath the sign!"

"Well, maybe it disappeared after your jog and before I came here?" Sonny says.

"I don't believe you, but it's okay." Charmin grabs me, walking away from the stand. "It's okay. Karma will get yo ass!"

"Have a good day, now!" Sonny smiles, waving us off with a smirk.

"Where we goin'?" I say in confusion.

"We need to do something." She takes me over to the other side of the street away from him.

"You right, but what?" Charmin and I stop for a moment to put our brains together. It wouldn't be hard to go vandalize his stand. Never the type to do something crazy like that, but I am the first to bring up the craziest ideas. Then again, what we do can't be on some rambunctious stuff. We know he took our sign down --- or at least, she knows he took our sign down. Charmin never lies and he did look and sound suspicious in a sneaky, lowkey way.

"I got it," says Charmin. "You know I help at the neighborhood clubhouse and I'm real cool with the neighborhood association. Let's go down to the clubhouse, speak to the neighborhood association manager, and get them to have him removed."

"You sure we should do all that?"

"Yes we should. We know he took our poster down. I swear it was nice and perfectly placed underneath the stop sign this morning. The only logical answer is him," Charmin says, ready to go ahead with the plan.

"Okay!" I say in a high-pitch, doubtful voice. As much as I want to take this man down, I don't want to cause any trouble for him. When I think of this plan, I think he is about to get taken down, arrested again, go to jail for breaking probation, and he is just a guy, trying to be better.

We walk past him again, not much to say as we walk by slowly. A drive-by on foot. I didn't look near his way, but Charmin's face was aimed at him all the way, ready to shoot if he made any move. We crossed the street and walked down the hill to the clubhouse. A five-house walk to get to the clubhouse from our street. Entering the clubhouse, we see that the pool is filled with kids, running around and jumping, splashing water and yelling while the lifeguard is chillin' on her stand. More children and families are walking in with their inflatable tubes and noodles. Seeing the people in the clubhouse tells me two things: Everybody in the neighborhood is out today and the association manager has to be here. We walk toward the side of the offices. One side of the clubhouse is the pool and the fitness center while the other side is the offices and main room. Charmin walks in the main room with no one in sight and no one on duty in the offices.

"Hold on, let me go ask Zoe."

"Who's Zoe?" I ask.

"She's the lifeguard at the pool and she helps me with the kids."

We walk outside to the pool. One kid's jump in the pool almost gets me wet, but I continue behind her in fear of getting wet. As she's walking to Zoe, a couple of children run to Charmin, happy as can be. All of them jump on her legs with their wet swim trunks and bathing suits. "Hey, Charmin!!!!!"

"Well, hello, my babies! Y'all look adorable in your swimwear. Y'all having fun?" Charmin says in her baby voice, hugging every one of them like a mother.

"Yeahhhhh!!!" The kids all try to tell her about one another with what games they are playin', who's it, what they have on, etc. With a child's heart, nothing can seem to get them down.

Charmin listens to the kids' chatter for a moment and says, "Hey guys! Y'all remember the street I live on?"

All the children nod their heads in synchronization, smiling at Charmin. "Well, if you have time after the pool, tell your parents to take you to the yard sale on that street. They may have some stuff for you to get. Can y'all do that for me, please?"

"Yeahhhhhh!!!!"

"Spread the word too. I'll see y'all later. Goodbye, my babies!" Charmin hugs them and waves as they run off.

After leaving the children, we walked to Zoe. Charmin goes to her and says, "Wassup, girl."

"Nothing, just waitin' til 3 to get off. Wassup with you?" she says, looking at me in a weird way.

"Oh nothin', girl. That Sonny dude did the most this morning.

He took down our yard sale sign underneath the street stop sign and set up his lemonade stand."

"Girl, for real?? How rude," says Zoe with the utmost bitterness. "So whatchu' gonna do?"

"Girl, we came here to try to get Magic on his ass, but it looks like he's not here."

"Yeah, girl, he's not here. They didn't have anything goin' on today, so he took off."

Charmin claps her hand. "Damnnn! Okay, thanks girl."

"Of course. Y'all should come back to the pool. It will probably be more chill once these children get tired and take their naps."

"Okay, cool." Charmin leads me out the gates of the clubhouse and we come back to square one, thinking of a better plan. As we think, I see a man walking on the sidewalk near the clubhouse. A man that looks familiar. Charmin looks over and recognizes him.

"Josh, that's Mr. Luther, the guy you were 'painting the picture' with the other day."

Looking at him closely, I see it is him and he looks like a man on a mission with the way he is walking in the direction of our street. Thinking of a solution scenario, I leave Charmin off impulse and run to him.

"Mr. Luther, Mr. Luther!" I yell. "Excuse me!"

He stops and looks at me, wondering who I am. Once I reach closer to him, his eyes get big, ready to talk before I can say something.

"Say, man, I called you this morning and you didn't pick up!"

"I'm so sorry, sir. We have been real busy." Charmin walks up behind me.

"It's all fine, I guess," he says.

"Are you walking to the yard sale?"

"I am. I figured I get my daily walk and see all that you were talkin' about. The neighborhood is live today, so I might as well refresh myself with all this bubbly energy."

"Of course! Nothing better than a lovely wake up to the neighborhood. It's funny because when we started our yard sale at nine, I don't think the neighborhood was awake then. Nobody was coming down our street or coming to the yard sale. To try to wake the neighborhood up, we wanted to walk to the end of our street and get our customers, but this Sonny dude took our Yard Sale sign down and put his lemonade stand in place of our street. Right now, we are trying to find a way to get him on another street and we believe you can help us." Charmin side-eyes me in a in a weird way, but I hold my ground and shush her mouth just in case she tries to intervene. Meanwhile, the man looks at me and begins to laugh.

"Now how can I help you? What this has to do with me?"

"It has nothing to do with you, but it can be once you walk up there with us, act like you're the association manager, tell him he doesn't have a license to sell lemonade on this street, and walk with us to the yard sale, where I will let you get one thing free."

The man looks at me with a pondering face, staring at my dignity and the sincerity in my eyes.

"Any one thing whether it's big or small?" he says, rubbing his chin.

"Any one thing," I say with a firm voice, bringing my hand out to shake like the one neighbor did to Charmin the other day. The man looks at my hand and then looks at my eyes, snickering just a little. Then he smiles and shakes my hand. Charmin wraps her arms around my shoulders and smirks at me, believing this plan might work. We walk up the street, seeing Sonny's lemonade stand in sight. He is jubilant and happy as he was this morning, but little does he know that we are about to rain on his parade.

The man walks tall to Sonny with us behind him. A weapon in stature.

"How you doing, my good man?" Sonny says, smiling.

"I'm doing good, but you are not," Mr. Luther says with professionalism.

"Excuse me?" Sonny says in confusion.

"According to the homeowner's code, you cannot solicit in front of a stop sign, especially if it impedes the stop sign for our drivers. In the next five minutes, you will need to break down this lemonade stand or your household will be fined $500 and I know your parents do not want to pay that." Official as a whistle when Mr. Luther said all this. Now I see why he almost sweet-talked me of his things. The man's serious face just surprises me. Sonny stands there in silence, depleted by his order. He then looks at us, and puts the two togethor, turning purple like grape Juicy Juice.

"Yes sir. I appreciate it," he says with a clenching smile.

Mr. Luther and I walk with Charmin, staring him down with an evil grin. It feels good to me, but it's something in the back of my mind telling me this was a bad idea; however, I walk with the man, gassin' him up like a balloon.

"So do you want to work for us on the yard sale too? You might bring in all the sales," I say, boosting him. On the spot, he played the association manager so well, making me feel scared for him.

"I knew we had a deal, so I had to fulfill my end of the bargain," says Mr. Luther, smiling and feeling himself.

"Wait!!!" Charmin halts, stopping us in our tracks. "I'm 'bout to go back to the front and get everybody to come down our street. I think I left my poster board and marker up there anyways."

"Okay, you sure? Sonny may still be up there."

"Man, Sonny ain't gonna do shit," Charmin says with sass. "Just watch as I get us some customers." And she walks off. Two snakes ready to rattle if need be. I just hope she is sure of herself.

When Charmin walks off, Mr. Luther and I head to the tables and look around for stuff that may interest him. He sees some jewelry, picking up a couple of our old watches from time to time. The baseball cards strike him a couple times, looking through their statistics and the feel of the cards. What grabs his attention the most is the old school recorder and some of the records. Sleek in style, he is in lure of the touch.

"Yo, my man! How much is the recorder?"

I look at Charles for the answer and he says a hundred dollars.

"What about the records?" he continues.

"Ten to twenty dollars."

The man grabs the recorder and a couple vinyl records and goes to Charles to pay.

"How you doin', sir?" Charles says with a small smile.

"I'm doin' good. Just glad to be out on a nice Saturday in the neighborhood."

Charles says "I feel you," doing calculations on his phone and summing up his cost.

"Okay sir, that will be $120."

The man laughs and then looks at me for assurance. "Well, my good man, your partner here told me I can get any one thing free before coming over here, so I want to get this recorder free."

"He said what?!!" Charles says, looking at me with rage.

I look at him with a fearful smile, saying, "He is right."

Charm notices the quarrel that is about to take place between Charles and me, so she steps in and tells us to talk to the side. She smiles at the man and begins talking to him.

"Nigga have you lost yo' mind?! Do you know how much money I had to save to get that recorder?!"

Trying to calm Charles down, I say "Sorry" about a hundred times before I can explain.

"Look! Hear me out! I made him a promise that he can get any one thing free if he did this one favor for me and Charmin."

"What favor, Josh?!"

"I'll tell you later, Charles. Please just understand me! I gotchu'! I'll tell you the whole thing later! In the meantime, I got about $200 saved up in the stash. If you need money, you can get that," I say, bringing his blood pressure down with my words and hands. I try to give him a hug for comfort, but he slings me off of him.

"Damnnn, Josh!" he says, grabbing his head. "Go grab $120 out your stash and give it to me, so we can put it in our money pouch."

"Okay." I run in the house, dashing upstairs to my room. A power couple lifts of the mattress and I reach under my bed for the shoe box that is my savings account and make a withdrawal. Running back outside to the driveway, the man smiles as if he just made a happy transaction with Charles.

"Nice doing business. Y'all have a good day!"

He walks off with the shiny recorder and records. It is a long walk back to his house. A part of me hopes that he makes it back safely while another part of me hopes somebody robs him and returns the stuff to us.

Charm goes over and talks to Charles, making sure he is okay. He seems to be bothered because not many customers came by and it didn't help having the man basically get his things for free.

"Don't give up yet, Charles. It's about late noon right now." Charm says.

"Beep! Beep!" Swerving all our heads to see where the beeps are coming from.. Five cars drive around the cul de sac and park on the curbs illegally, blocking some of the entrances for our neighbors and their driveways. Every car door opens, with kids jumping out of their seats, excited to come over to the yard sale. Looking closely, it's the same little kids from the pool, wild and ready. The parents come out, doing all they can to calm down their kids, but they look excited to see the yard sale. Charles perks up from his chair while Charm turns up the speaker and grabs most of the children to go dance with her.

Looking down the street near the stop sign, I see more people walking in this direction. Charles begins to perk up and trot back to the tables. Moms come to him about the necklaces and rings for sale. Dads come to me about the records and old appliances. Charm dances and plays with the kids with rugrat games. The first game is tag and the second game is invisible hula-hoop; laughing as I think about the made-up games you create as a kid. I take a stand near the register for help once I am done helping the dads. Searching in the crowd of customers, I don't see many of the homeowners that I talked to the other day. The demographic appears more new faces than familiar ones. As I'm scanning, I see a scenario take place where one of the kids is loving the baseball cards, holding Dad's vintage Satchel Paige and Hank Aaron limited editions to light and digging in his pockets for some change. He then looks for his mother, but she is mesmerized by the cherry red heels on the table. Reading his lips, he says, "Mom, can I get these?" The mom is intertwined with the heels, taking them out and trying on one of the heels. They look good on her as I'm overlooking her style. The mom puts the shoes back in the box and gets the cards as well, not even giving a chance for the kid to beg and comes to me.

"Is that it?" I say as I grab the stuff. She nods yes as the kid can't wait to have his cards.

Doing the math behind the table, I say, "That will be $100."

The mom looks at me with a stank look. "$100?! How much are the cards?"

"$25 each, ma'am," I say, looking at the kid.

"Can we get it, Mom? Please Mom pleasssssssssssssse!!!!" the kid says with puppy dog eyes. Hard to resist, the mom says yes. She reaches down her purse and gives me the money. The kid bounces like a spring with joy as they go back to the car, creating a sweet moment for the day, it makes me glad to see the yard sale sparking sales. A couple of times, Charles and I switch positions to where I talk to customers and he is the cashier. As time goes, items go one by one from the table. Kids and cars leave the cul de sac one-by-one. After I get done with escorting one customer to Charles, I see Vickie walking up to me.

"Well, hello, Vickie!" I say with jubilance.

"Hello, Josh. How are you?"

"Well, as you can see. . ." I say with my arms out, showing her the scene. "I'm doin' good. What about you?"

"Well, I was in the neighborhood and my chakras gave me a

reminder to come today."

"I'm glad it did. If you see anything you like, just let me know."

"Okay." Vickie walks around and looks at our things. I wish Charmin was here for her to see Vickie since she helped her with the bee sting. Browsing through, she toys with the jewelry, fumbling with each jewel. Next to it, she feels the fabric of the clothes, looking at the tags as she feels the material. The way she looks through our stuff makes me think we do have some luxures. She continues to smile when she sees some of the appliances, but she doesn't get stunned until she sees Charles' art collection. Amazed by the art work, she begins to thumb through the pieces, looking at each one in wonder and curiosity. Charm taps my brother to peep the way Vickie is looking at his stuff, shoo'ing him to walk over to her.

"What do you think about these pieces?" Charles says to her.

Vickie looks at him speechless, trying to find the words to say to him.

"Wow.... all I can really say is wow."

"What do you like about them?" he asks.

Vickie puts the pieces down with such care. "The message behind each painting speaks to the chaos that is in this country. Looking at these pieces, I can see the racial undertone. For example, this one." She grabs the piece he made the other night in the basement. "The black lines rain over the canvas with the white office desk. Just looking at the whole piece, I hear the voice of how there are million. Speaks to how there are a million black employment candidates worthy of the jobs they apply in America; like literally raining from the grey sky. Yet, the white office desk is a symbol to the conservative values of corporate America. With the black man falling from the desk chair, it's a fall that is hard for him to get up because the people who sit at the white desk want to keep him down there."

"That's interesting you say that," my brother says. "I made that piece the other day after I got fired from my job. The black lines represent chaos, but the grey sky represents the storm that will weather on corporate America when it includes black employees.

I thought more so as a storm because once there is one successful black employee, there will be another and another and another, causing white employers to be scared or accept the diversity. It brings a question to the white employees whether they see us more as a storm or beautiful weather from Mother Nature."

Vickie nods her head at Charles, loving his response while continuing to look at his piece again.

"So why do you include the black man falling from the chair?" she asks.

"So the black man falling is the result of the storm, causing him to fall because once more employees of color come, then a certain expectation and standard is raised. For some workers of color, they rise to the standard and continue to do a good job. For others, they fall or slip to the standard, causing them to lose their job."

"Wow, that's powerful. You made the other ones too besides the Basquiat pieces?"

"Yes I did," Charles says with pride. It makes me happy to know how my brother makes time to paint even when he comes back from tours.

Vicky counts with her finger how many canvases my brother has and asks, "How much are the paintings?"

Charles looks at her in a questionable way. "Do you mean all together or the price for each?"

"All together." Vickie says the phrase in a low volume, but somehow Charm and I hear her over the speaker and the kids playing. A seismic wave once she ended her sentence. Charles yells at me with conviction.

"Yo Josh! Help her carry these paintings to the front so we can give her a cost." He gives me a look that says this is a good sale.

I walk over to collect the paintings, smiling at her as I gather them all together. Vickie smiles back in a cool way. Lifting the paintings is heavy duty as I bring them to the cashier part of the table, so I know it will be a load for her.

"Charles! We may need that cart buggy out here and have her take the paintings in that."

Charles salutes me with his thumbs up and goes to the garage to get it. As he is going over to get it, I don't say anything to Vickie because the words are written all over my face. Buying the paintings is a big deal for Charles and it can encourage him to paint and sell more of his work. Vickie stands and smiles with gratitude. Charles brings the cart buggy and rolls around to put the paintings in the buggy. When finished, he comes back around to put in calculations for the artwork.

"Okay, ma'am, that will be $200."

Vickie smiles in astonishment and begins to take her checkbook out, putting it down on the table. She takes out her pen and then looks at the pieces and Josh for clarity, twiddling the pen with her fingers. After a couple of spins with her fingers, she raises up.

"How about this? How about I give you $5,000 for all the pieces and how about you do me a favor?"

Charles' eyes widen, as if her words inflate his pupils while inflating my excitement. "What favor do you need?" Charles asks.

"So this morning, I have gotten a commission to do a mural on the playground wall in the neighborhood. I didn't think it was going to be a bad idea to do it myself, but after seeing your work, I would love for you to work with me on creating the mural."

Ohhhhh snap! I think, wondering why it is taking him so long to say yes. Charles' face is ecstatic and in disbelief, but he prolongs his best imitation of the Thinker sculpture. It's a no brainer of what he should say. Why is he taking so long?

"What is your name, ma'am?" he says.

"Victoria Martin, but you can call me Vickie," she says, sticking her hand out to shake.

"Well, I'm in the midst of finding a job because I just got fired from my corporate job, so I don't know if I will have time to help you on the mural."

Vickie smiles with joy and says, "It's all good. You can get half of the commission money working with me. I believe the neighborhood association is putting up $15,000 to paint the mural by the end of the summer. Would $8,000 be fine with you?"

Once again the pondering face is killing me. The nerve in my vocal chord gives me the reflex to say "That's fine" as if I were his agent, but I try to control my excitement. Charm looks back and walks over just in time to see what we are doing.

"What's goin' on, guys?"

"You tell me, bro?" I say with contention. Charles ignores me and taps his foot with his arms folded to think of another question to ask. Charm walks over to me and whispers to me for answers. I tell the magic information in her ear like the telephone game. As soon as she hears it, she loses it.

"Boy! You betta' take that money. Why you stallin' her?!" Charm blurts out, giving Charles the third degree.

Excuse me. He will gladly accept. Right, Charles? Charles plays it tough begins to smile and hug Vickie with endearment. A gesture that agrees to do the mural. A lituation on the spot. Charm and I cheer for him in the background, excited for him to have the opportunity since getting fired. They exchange contact information, chat for a little while, and she begins to push her buggy full of his work home. On the cusp of leaving, she turns around and asks, "What do you call the name of the one piece you did this week?"

Charles scratches his chin with a little grin and says, "Stormy weather!"

Vickie chuckles, smiling at the answer, and walks off. Charm and I come over to congratulate him, jumping on his back, giving him hugs, feeding his ego until his ego stomach pops, and everything in between. Five minutes later, Charmin comes back from the front of the street with exhaustion on her face, drenched in sweat and a loss of breath. Once we tell her the news, she gives him the driest hooray with a sandy voice.

Charm checks the time and notices that the majority of the

things from the table are gone, hinting at Charles to shut it down. Charles agrees with her and we all pack up the items and place them back in the basement. Charmin has little to no energy to give, so we suggest that she bring some popsicles from her house to us. She runs along to get them with the little energy she has, knowing that she is the MVP of the day. After cleaning up the driveway and clearing things away, we all meet at the powerbox in the cul de sac. I heard it's something about that green rectangle where the wires and the electricity inside of it configures light-bulb ideas for the next move.

We knew we had to celebrate, which is why we didn't want to meet at our house. Thinking of ideas within an air conditioned confinement is sleepily dangerous. We needed a plan before we adjourned. "Look, I know everybody is tired and what not, but we need to do something to celebrate this occasion," says Charm, commanding our attention. "What about a kickback or a party?"

"Oooooh, a party sounds real good to me." I sit back and think. Knowing that I have never been to one, but Charles shoots it down with ease.

"Y'all want to go get pizza or ice cream?" Charm asks. Charles shakes his head in disagreement again, making Charm become irritated.

"Well, Charles, we need to do something!" Charm emphasizes.

"What time is it right now?" Charles asked.

"6:30," I say.

"How about we go to the pool and chill there tonight?" Charmin says.

"Honestly, that sounds like the best move right now," Charles agrees. "Everybody go shower and change and we can ride down there in 30 minutes. Is that cool?"

Everyone says bet. Well barely due to Charm's insecurity about getting her hair wet. We all split from the powerbox, dragging our way to our houses. Snail pace. I shower first as Charles flops and passes out on his bed for a few minutes. Catching his breath to recuperate. I clean myself up quickly so I can save time to look at myself in the mirror. I critique my body to see if my muscles are good for the pool and Charmin. I notice that the flat chest needs to pop out, so I go back to the room and do a hundred pushups. Well, attempt to do it. Every pushup after thirty gets harder, so then I convert to girl pushups, using all my strength while it is easy. After I'm done, I walk to the bathroom again and see my arms are more toned and the bird chest I have is more protruded. I get some lotion so I can look defined. Every bodybuilder uses it, so why shouldn't I? Charles is ready by the time I get done oiling up. We walk downstairs and get in the car to go pick them up. When we come to their house, we chill for a second. Charles calls Charm and tells her we are outside. The door opens and then they come out like a runway model to the car. Charm walks out the house first with her silk satin robe and shades on; nice and glammed for the pool. Then Charmin comes out as I glue my eyes out the window to microscope her behind Charm. A floral fresh face battered with a little cake and blush, topped with a shiny smile with lips so plush; not to forget her silky skin that glosses with her butterfly wing pattern two-piece bathing suit, making me want to wrap her up like a cocoon when she gets in the car. I'm biting my lip as she walks to the car, making sure I'm sitting in a good posture for her to notice this gun show. She comes to my side and I scoot over with all eyes on her. Charmin puts her belongings on the floor and looks at me with peculiarity, noticing my face.

"You okay?"

Stuck in my words as if she made me lose air to say something, I just nod and look out the window. So many thoughts come to my mind when we drive off. The other day Charles said he's glad my summer is going well. The fact that Charmin is sitting with me in her two-piece to go to the pool is a fine example of a great summer, but I'm glad his summer is changing gears for the better as well. Maybe it can switch his profession from the military to staying at home.

The Audition

The gang arrives at the clubhouse after cruising through a deep blue sky with starry street lights to guide the way. After parking, Charles and Charm get out of the car first with anticipation to relax and swim. Charmin gets out of the car, begging Charm to take her picture for the 'Gram. Josh notices her attention toward the picture, debating if he wants to photobomb it as he walks slowly in the frame of the picture. Charmin feels his shadow and looks at him with indifference, moving him to the side.

Cheese!

They walk into the clubhouse and see the pool area is clear, making Charles feel ecstatic as he fist pumps into the air. Charm takes another picture for Charmin along the poolside lounge chair with Charm's shades and her robe, using all the props to make the picture fabulous. From afar, Josh looks and ignores his impulse to try to be in the picture again. Dropping his bag by Charles' chair, Josh trots to the deep end and belly flops into the pool. Falling and clapping into his water bed, he sinks and swims to the shorter end of the pool. Charles runs from his chair and front flips into the pool, splashing water near a careful Charm. The flip is a ten from his splash and his diving form. He raises to the top and yells at Charm to get in, but she rejects his call and chills in her lounge chair. Charmin gives back Charm's props for her 'Gram photo and then puts her hair in a bun. Walking over to the deep end, she does a perfect backflip into the pool. A ten for style and grace. She comes up like a swan out of the water. Majestic in all senses, as Josh notices, chillin in the three-foot end entranced by her. Charles swims over to Josh and says, "Yo, Josh, I got a plan," whispering to him in a conniving way. The two discuss their plan, using the chlorine water as their drawing board and chuckling softly to solidify the plan. Breaking it down with a fist bump, Josh goes to the bathroom and Charles swims to the side nearest to Charm.

"So you really gonna stay in that chair all night? You have a scarf and a swim cap on," Charles says, but Charm doesn't mind his words.

"Look! This is how I have fun at the pool and that is how you have fun at the pool. Can I live?"

"Okay I feel you, but come here. I need to tell you something."

Charm looks at Charles funny. "Whatchu' need to tell me? You can tell me from right there."

"Charm for real! It's about them two." Charles points at Charmin and Josh discreetly. Charm rolls her eyes and gets up carefully from her chair, walking slowly and with suspicion as she kneels down to talk to Charles.

"Wassup?" she says as Charles laughs and comes closer.

"Yo! Guess who hittin' who from the back?"

Charm's face turns red, going from 0 to 100 in a heartbeat.

"Who the fuck hittin' WHO from the back?!" Charm yells with aggression, leaning like the tower in Europe. Josh awkwardly tiptoes behind Charm and yells "Me!" as he thrusts his hips behind her with force, knocking her momentum forward into the water. Josh and Charles high-five each other, laughing at her. Charm splashes violently; a fiery Free Willy raging in and out of the water. Similar to a cat that's not ready to bathe. She loses it, jumping at Charles, and they wrestle in the water. Charmin sees the action and swims over to the madness to jump Charles. Josh sees her coming to help and hesitates on jumping in. Once Charles sees him, he says, "Really, bro?!"

Josh takes a deep sigh and rescue leaps at Charmin, splashing her off of Charles and into the water. Two quarrels are happening in the pool with no lifeguard or audience in sight. Josh takes on Charmin until Charmin jumps on his back and takes him down. Charles rises from Charm's choke slam, bellowing out the water like a whale. Neither person stops or loses will, fighting to the death that is close to drowning. The fighting doesn't simmer down until a family walks in, observing the chaos. Charm in mid-action sees the family and commands the horseplay of Charles to stop, tilting his body toward their direction so he can see them. Charles catches a glimpse of the family and stops. Charmin and Josh continue to go at it until Charm yells "Stop!" freezing them in their stance.

"Is everything okay?" the mother says, hiding her son behind her leg.

"Yeah, we're fine," says Charm, getting ready to come out of the pool and sit back in her chair. Charles walks out of the pool with her and pulls his chair up to hers. Charmin and Josh continue to swim toward the mother, apologizing and if it is cool to play Marco Polo with their son.

The father agrees as the child hurries, throwing his bag down and ready to jump in the pool.

Charles sits next to Charm with caution, knowing that she has ill feelings toward him.

"Boy, don'tchu ever do that again." she says, punching him in the arm.

"Owwww!" Charles says, grabbing his arm.

"But it's okay. I'mma get you back. Trust and believe that." They both look at the Marco Polo action in the pool, laughing off some steam with the trickery of the little kid and Charmin as Josh tries to find them. Yelling "Polo" on one side of the pool as Charmin and the kid swims the speed of light to elude a blind Josh looking for them.

"Okay for real though. What do you think about today?" Charm asks.

"Honestly, I can't believe it. The way it was lookin' this morning didn't seem like we were goin' to have much success. Then all of a sudden, customers came, kids came, and then the next thing you see is most of the stuff gone. We really made some money today, Charm."

"Oh yeah, the yard sale was crazy, but how you feel about the lady and her buying your pieces and offering you a job?"

"Is it really a job though?" Charles questions.

"Man, you gettin' paid, so YES!"

"I don't know; it just all felt surreal. One minute she's looking at my pieces and the next minute she's talkin' bout giving me $5,000 for it. It was crazy too because this white lady really had a lot to say about my painting. Definitely the eccentric type to have all those tattoos and walk back to her house with a buggy full of the paintings," Charles says, laughing.

"But why did it take you that long to answer?"

"Because I didn't want it to be a scam or it was just all talk. After I agreed with her on the mural, she showed me how she is over this non-profit called Drink My Paint."

Charm laughs after hearing the name. "What do they do besides drink paint?"

"You stupid." Charles giggles. "But nah. She said it's a way where she hosts sip-n-paint parties for impoverished kids. Plus, instead of having a piece to follow, they draw whatever comes to mind when she presents them with a story. Then she said she would buy the paintings and make a collage out of them and put it in a museum every other month."

"Wow, that's dope. See! We have all the connections in the neighborhood and yeen even know it."

"I guess." Charles shrugs. "All this talent that people rarely see out here."

"Exactly. Speaking of talent, guess what?"

"What?" Charles leans closer.

"Man, you're supposed to guess!"

"Ummmm. Wait, would it have anything to do with your dance group?"

"Hell yeah!" Charm yells. "We got an audition to be in No Cap Nate's new music video tomorrow!"

"Yoooooo! Word?! Awwwwww Charm, that's finna be lit!" says Charles, hugging her in excitement. "Like how did y'all get that set up?"

"So before you came back, we had this little performance at the skating rink before closing and we brought the house down. Having all the middle school kids lit and just in awe. So like once we were about to leave, the owner of the Skating Rink wanted our number for more Friday night performances. I gave him mine and then three weeks later, he's tellin' me No Cap Nate needs some dancers."

"Dangggg! That's crazy. So are y'all ready for tomorrow?" Charles ask.

Charm smacks her teeth in disgust. "Man, Charles, I hope so. Me and Tiffany gonna be straight. It's just that Sade be the main crack in the group. She always be doin' the most. I mean she's the best dancer and all, but she is not the group. Thinkin' she's Destiny and I'm her child. Plus, she be trippin' too."

"Well, she'll probably be good tomorrow. We talkin' bout No Cap Nate. This a big opportunity right here."

"Yeah, I hope so."

Charles gets up from his chair.

"Wait! So when are you supposed to start?" Charm asks.

"She told me Monday. I think we are going to go over ideas and brainstorm first," Charles says, getting ready to go back into the pool. Charm relaxes in her chair, humming the song of No Cap Nate's new song "Fasho." After hangin' in the pool, the gang drives back and knocks out cold. Something about pool water that makes you sleep after a swim. Charm goes to sleep with excitement, yet anticipation for a big day tomorrow.

● ⋯⋯⋯⋯⋯⋯● ⋯⋯⋯⋯⋯ ●

"Clack, clack, clack!"

Charm nudges a little bit, turning over in her covers to find that comfortable position.

"Clack, clack, clack!"

A deep sigh is her reaction as Charm puts the pillow over her head, but not all the way because she doesn't want to press down on her hair.

"Clack, clack, clack!"

A mummy from the dead, Charm raises out of bed wondering about the noise as she begins to take her sleep eye mask off. Climbing out of her heart-shaped comfy bed, she grabs her robe and puts her slippers on, walking out of her room and into the hallway.

"Clack, clack, clack!"

Snoozing down the hallway, she checks Charmin's room and wonders why she doesn't hear the sound. Peeking through her bedroom door, Charm notices that Charmin fell asleep again with her headphones in her ears. Most likely, she was listening to Beyonce.

"Clack, clack, clack,clack,clack!" It gets louder.

Agitated by the noise, she hurries up walking downstairs, so this person can make no more knocks. She opens up the door and finds no one in sight. Stepping onto the outside doormat, she searches both ways to see if there is anybody playing jokes. Furious to see no one, she slams the door and marches back upstairs, yawning as she makes her way. She takes off her robe and slippers and falls back into bed, cuddling the comforters to help alleviate her irritated mood.

"Clink!"

"What was that?" Charm asks herself, opening her eyes. Holding herself still, she pauses her breath, her stomach, and her mind to find the distinct location of the sound.

"Clink!"

Charm's ears detect the window as the first location. Opening her curtains, she looks outside and sees Sade picking up rocks in her front yard. Bangin' on the window to get Sade's attention, she yells, "Whatchu' want?!"

Sade gives a sign language to come downstairs, walking to her front door. Charm puts back on her robe and her slippers with irritation and stomps her way downstairs, giving each stair step more pain.

Charm opens her door. "Sade, it is seven in the freakin' morning! Why are you disturbing my sleep at seven in the morning?!" Charm says, restraining herself to snap.

"Because girl we need to talk!" Sade projects, out-matching her tone and volume.

"Well you couldn't wait 'til 12?!"

"Nope," Sade says, with her arms crossed around her chest.

Charm rolls her eyes, inviting her into the house. They walk into the living room and sit on the couch. "So what's up?"

"Yo, wassup with your little sister, girl?"

"Whatchu' mean?! What she do?" Charm asks, boiling up a sweat.

"She shut down my little brother's hustle!"

"Still whatchu' mean? What she do?"

Directing angry traffic with her hands, she says, "She got the neighborhood association to shut down his lemonade stand. Now he can't sell lemonade any more."

"Okay and what that have to do with me?" Charm says with a zesty lack of care.

"That means we ain't gettin' no side money in the house. Now how the fam gon' eat?! How I'm gonna eat?!" Sade says, distraught.

"It's not me, it's her. Whatchu' want me to do?"

"Get her ass to apologize and get the people to let him sell lemonade again. Everybody was rockin' with the lemonade too. Let me tell you girl how that juice can make the heaven gates in your mouth sing a ratchet girl hymn after one taste."

"Okay! Okay! But Charmin wouldn't do something like this for no reason. What makes you think he didn't cause the problem?"

Sade smacks her teeth with assertion. "Psscht. Because he's the sweetest now. He's not like before, so I'mma need you to see wassup with your sister."

"Fine, girl, fine. I'll see wassup, but are you ready for today?!" Charm asks with excitement.

"Girl yassssssssss!! Once we kill this audition, I'mma ask the director if I can dance next to No Cap Nate, heyyyyyyy. Throwin' all the ass on him too from his shoe strings to his forehead," Sade says, chuckling with Charm as they laugh it up.

"Girl, you stupid, but okay cool," Charm says, getting ready to get up from the couch.

"Hold on, real quick. So on the last hook section, can we incorporate this move?" Sade hits the dance floor that is the carpet and cuts a rug with her routine, starting with a couple shoulder shimmies. Then slide to the left, slide to right. Pop the shoulder left and then swing it to the right. Drop to the floor, twerk it on the knees, end with a wink so the judges can be pleased. There you have it. Sade gets up from the floor, wiping her head and fixing her hair after finishing the routine. "Girl, whatchu' think?"

"Girl, hell naw!" Charm says, rejecting her dance. "Girl, let's just stick to the routine and worry about doin' the fundamentals. Showin' them we can incorporate the modern with some contemporary."

"Girl, I feel you, but we got to leave something for them to hold on when we're done, though. Just like I did at the skating rink," Sade says back.

"Girl, they not lookin' for the booty-shakin stuff. How many times do I have to tell you that? Once we get in through our dance routine first, then we can do all the booty-shakin we want. Don't forget, Sade, this ain't the skating rink. This No Cap Nate."

Sade rolls her eyes with disappointment. "Okay fine, but ask Tiffany and see what she thinks," she says as she gets ready to leave the house. "Don't forget, Charm, talk to your sister."

"Okay, girl. Don't forget to come to my house at twelve. I expect to see you and Tiffany on time."

Sade says okay and leaves the house. Closing the door, Charm goes upstairs and quietly goes into Charmin's room. Tiptoeing to her night stand, she slowly lifts the headphones out of Charmin's ears and puts one in her ear. Charm makes a hard snicker once she hears "Me, Myself, and I" by Beyonce on low volume. A classic anthem that can explain most girls' stories of their life. Charm goes to open her blinds with little sunlight to make an entrance through the window. Cloudy skies in the atmosphere, but Charm expects to have a great day. Walking toward Charmin sound asleep in bed, she bugs and tugs her shoulder. Each tug makes Charmin look like a dead person.

"Charmin, wake up!" Charm yells. Charmin begins to move in spurts until Charm shoves her hard, knocking Charmin's head into the headboard. Hitting it real hard, Charmin wakes up, singing, "All the ladies, if you feel me, help me sing it out!" and then closes her mouth, feeling embarrassed as Charm rolls on her bed, laughing it up.

"Stop laughing," Charmin says, stretching her arms and wiping her eyes.

"Oh so that's how you feelin' these days with Beyonce?" Charm says, giggling.

"Whatchu' mean?"

"Me, Myself, and I? All that time you be hangin' with Josh and you bumpin' me, myself, and I?"

Charmin gives a heavy sigh, rolling her eyes to the foolery Charmin speaks. "Girl, you tellin' me you woke me up early this morning to tell me this?"

"No, but at least play Love on Top or Party (I told my girls you can get it)." Charmin sings at the end.

"Pschht, girl, whatchu' wake me up for? You know I don't go to the clubhouse today."

"I know, I know, but I just needed to ask you a question. Sade came running to me, talkin' bout how you shut down her little brother lemonade stand."

"That's her little brother?!" Charmin says, startling herself from what Charm tells her.

"Yeah, Charmin. So what happened?"

"Honestly sis, it was his fault. It was yesterday too. Remember when me and Josh left to go show people the posters of the yard sale?"

"Yeah."

"Well when we walked up to go post up at the stop sign, this man took down the poster I had attached below the stop sign and set up his lemonade stand instead. Honestly, he prolly' was the reason why we didn't have customers at first because he would get them all first and then direct them to another street."

"Wait, so you walked up and literally saw him taking down the yard sale sign and posting up his lemonade stand?"

Charm hesitates with a pause. "Well, not exactly."

"Hold on now. Tell the truth, Charmin. Did you see this man take down the sign?"

Charmin blushes with a grin. "No."

Charm throws her hands up in disbelief. "Damn, Charmin. So you the reason why Sade comin' over here early, throwin' a tantrum."

"I'm sorry, Charm and why she do all that? See, you need to let her ass go. Actin' like she Beyonce when she's Michelle. You know it ain't a thing for me to join the group," says Charmin, tugging on Charm's arm.

"Charmin, stop," she says, pulling her arm away. "You need to go over there and apologize to that boy. And you really got the association people to say that he can't sell lemonade no more?"

"Technically no. We just got one of our customers to pretend to be an association person and scare him. All that stuff isn't real."

"Well, go apologize to that little boy, NOW!"

Charmin smacks her teeth in disgust. "Calm down, calm down. Can I do it by the end of the day? Sheesh, at least let me do it after y'all kill the audition."

Charm mean mugs at her and says fine.

"Okay, thank you. I gotchu'. Just focus on getting this audition and I will do it afterwards," Charmin says, laying back down into her bed to catch more z's.

Charm leaves and goes back into her room to try to do the same, but she struggles to fall back asleep. Due to all the madness that happened this morning, she goes downstairs and gets a cup of orange juice. She sits at the kitchen table as she thinks about the audition today. Humming No Cap Nate's new song, she gulps her cup of orange juice and takes out her phone. Scrolling to his new song, she plays it and goes in the middle of the living room to dance. An imaginary crowd on the couch as her audience, Charm performs. Swaying from left to right before the beat drops. Five, six, seven, eight. She begins head bopping to the left with a shoulder jerk to the right. Leaning to the left and back to the right, clapping her feet on the ground to the syncopation of the trap-influenced beat. Her feet clap in a circle around the living room. A Michael Jackson spin with a high-five to the left. A Michael Jackson spin with a high-five to the right. Transitioning into the hook of the song, she begins to incorporate the new popular dance out called the Scotch. A kidz bop frenzy that took over at the beginning of the summer. Charm starts the Scotch by throwing her hand out in front as if she is walking a dog. Then she hops in the imaginary carpet spots while jigging her shoulders to the beat, showing off her hops and balance in her slippers. After she comes onto her last hop, she picks up one foot and kicks it while the opposite foot hops, punching her fist while moving her elbow. Grooving into the next part, she double Dutches with a lean with it rock with it. Cabbage patch swirl with a Bruce Lee kick with it. Lastly, shimmying her shoulders with a Harlem shake on the side. She twerks it in and dips to the left. Twerk it out and dip to the right. A ballet hop back to the center, she poses with her hand on her hip and a fearsome face that gives you fever. She breathes smoothly in through her nose and out through her mouth, looking at the fireplace as if the director is there in the flesh. Silent with no response, Charmin breaks the silence clapping and yells, "Oh God! Lovely, Bravo, Encore!"

Hearing laughing at her from behind, Charm turns around to see Charmin.

"You did all that in a robe and some slippers, so imagine when you do it in leggings and sneakers?" Charmin says with an applauding smile.

Charm grins at Charmin, walking back into the kitchen to get some more juice.

The morning goes by fast as the anticipation to seize the audition arrives. Charm goes back to her room to get her mind off the pressure by watching television. A Sunday morning special, to be exact. Once the morning special is over, she hits the ground running, laying out her leggings and red top with the red shoes on the bed. Then, she showers and hurries back to dry smoothly, wrapping the towel around her hair and body. Once she settles, she goes to the sacred part of the room. A dim-lighted area that can be mistaken for a shrine, where a chair and table holds different stencils, different colored powders, different brushes and a centered mirror. A work of art on the canvas, she sits down and begins to bake her face with one of the brushes, capping it off with a stencil on her eyebrows and gloss for her lips. Next is blow drying her hair after unwrapping her hair towel. Then, it's getting dressed. Lastly, she waits for the girls to come to her house so she can drive them to the audition. A careful posture as she sits on the couch, making sure she is not leaning back so her hair stays in place.

"Clack, clack, clack!" The door knocks as Charm waits patiently in the living room. She walks to the door and opens it.

"Hey, girl!" Tiffany says, greeting her in a lively way.

"Hey, Tiffy!" They hug and walk into the living room, checking each other out on appearance.

"Girl, where's your comb at? Let me fix your hair," Tiffany says, running upstairs to her bathroom and back.

"Damn, Tiffy, I just did it. Sorry I can't get like you," Charm says.

"Girl, stop! It's just something small. That's it." Tiffany runs downstairs and sits Charm down to start.

"Girl, you ready?"

"Hell yeah, I'm ready. We're gonna steal the scene at this audition. I just hope Sade ready too."

Charm turns her head around, glaring at Tiffany in agreement. "Who you tellin'? Hold on, what time is it?"

Tiffany takes out her phone and says, "It's 11:15!"

"Okay. We good. She just needs to be here before we leave at 11:30," Charm decrees. Finishing up her hair, Tiffany shows Charm her mirror for approval.

"Damn Tiffy! See, this is why we friends. Always know how to come through." She turns around and high-fives her with a finger.

Time goes by and the smell of the fragrances used by Tiffany and Charm clears away the atmosphere, anticipation builds into the air as each minute gets closer to 11:30. Tiffany and Charm stay patient until Tiffany looks at her phone one last time.

"Girl, it's 11:30. Where the fuck is she?"

"Oh my God! Where is she?" Charm says, calling Sade on her phone. The phone rings and rings and ends with her voicemail, adding more fuel to the fire that steams for Sade. Tiffany sits on the couch with her arms crossed, looking at her phone to stall time. Charm sits next to her, tapping her leg in irritation. Scrolling on the Gram could not take her focus off Sade's tardiness.

"Forget it, girl. Let's bounce," Charm says out the blue with controlled rage.

"You sure, Charm?"

"Yes girl! I'm finna pull up and give it to her." She grabs Tiffany's hand and walks her to the front door to leave. Opening the door, Sade is standing, laughing with a rack of cups in her left hand and her phone in the right.

"Damn, y'all was going to leave me?!"

"Sade, do you know what time it is?!" Charm yells.

"Yeah it's..." Sade checks the phone and says "Ooops," laughing at her mistake. "Mybad. The only reason I was late is because I wanted to be considerate and bring y'all some of my brother's lemonade to calm our nerves."

"That's fine 'n all, but we have to go!" Charm says, pacing the way to the car. Sade and Tiffany follow behind her to get in.

"Damn, I said mybad. See, you definitely need this lemonade so you can relax. You not gonna make me tense before the audition." Charm looks at the cup, noticing the green exterior of the drink. She turns her back to face the street and drives off, saying, "I'm good."

"You sure? I'm tellin' you, girl. This stuff is good."

Charm nods her head in disgust, saying, "Yeah I'm sure."

Sade looks to Tiffany in the passenger seat for approval. "Girl, you want some? I got it for you."

"Ooooh, girl, I would, but I have to use the restroom, so I can't take another cup to drink right now," Tiffany says, squirming in her seat. "I'm sorry."

"Damn, y'all. The time I take to help my dance partners and y'all don't even take my offering," Sade says with salt.

"We gotchu' another time. Thing is, Sade, are you ready?"

Sade drinks all three of the cups, gulping all the drinks before she gives an answer. "Hell yeah, girl. This finna be a breeze. Buuuuuuuuuuuurp!" Sade giggles as Charm looks at her in distaste. "Excuse me."

Tiffany and Charm look at each other in unison through the front mirror in worry. Arriving at the audition in an eager manner,

Charm parks the car as Tiffany grabs her stuff and sprints to the audition desk to check in the group. Sade grabs her bag and hops out the car, so she can run to the waiting line. During mid-run, Sade trips on herself, falling in slow motion and coming down hard. The roll and tumble to the ground roughs up her outfit. No time to feel sorry, she dusts herself off and gets up with urgency to play off the embarrassing moment. Moving to take off to the line, she freezes, eyes turning back as goosebumps creep up her back. Sade grabs her chest in discomfort, feeling her heart beating heavy like congo. The veins in her skin began to throb uncontrollably and her hair poofs out of its relaxed and pressed state. Her hands tingle as if her nervous system pressed the wrong switch. Sade's trance loses her at a time where Charm does not notice. Ending her body spin cycle, she burps again, finding her way to move slowly. Charm sees her standing in an awkward stance and comes over.

"Sade, you okay?"

Sade looks at Charm with her eyes low and her arms wobbly as noodles. She holds on to Charm as a crutch for a little more strength.

"Sade?!" Charm lets her go with gradual care and Sade stumbles to hold herself up.

"C'mon, Sade. Stop playin'. You okay?"

Sade giggles at Charm's question and smiles. "Yasssssss I am. Are yuuuuuuuu okay?" The slur in her words confuses Charm, helping her along to the waiting line. Tiffany looks at Charm and Sade, puzzled by why she is helping Sade walk.

"Yo, what happened to her?"

"Girl, I don't know. She was running from my car. Next thing I know, I look and she's actin' like E.T."

Sade is oblivious to what Tiffany and Charm are saying as she plays with her face, smiling with her tongue out and constantly winking her eyes. Tiffany and Charm observe the weird behavior, sitting her down in the line to get her together.

"Yo, Tiffany! Fix her hair real quick." Tiffany grabs the comb out of her bag as Charm proceeds to talk to her. "Sade, are you good?

Can you dance? Talk to me."

"Yeahhhh girrrrrrl. Don't I look like it?" Sade walks out the line with irregular balance. Turning to Sade and Tiffany in a crooked stance, she smiles. "Five, six, fiiiive, six, seven, eight." She bops her head to left with a shoulder jerk to the right. She snaps her finger, but it doesn't make the timing right. With little balance, she leans to the left and leans to the right too hard, knocking herself back like an astronaut in space. The other dancers in the line snicker, putting their hands on their faces to hide their expressions. Charm gets out of line to grab her, dragging her back in line.

"Girl, what done happened? You were fine 'bout a minute ago," Tiffany says, freaking out. As Sade has her head down from the pull of Charm, she turns to Tiffany. "Girl, I'm finnnnnne. We just need to relaaaaaax," she says, letting her fingers drizzle down in front of Tiffany and Charm. Blowing her lips, she begins making sounds. "Brrrr, Brrrr, Brrrr, Eeeee, Eeeee, Eeeeee!" To shut out the noises, Charm puts her hand around Sade's mouth and tells her to stay put, grabbing Tiffany's hand and walking out of line to the side.

"Yo! What is goin' on? This not funny, Charm."

"I know, I know," she says, trying to comfort Tiffany in distress. "Look! I need you to go back, keep her cool until I get back."

"Where you goin'?"

"I'm goin' to find some aspirin and get a drink for her to take."

"You sure you should do this?" Tiffany says in caution. "We are like fifty people away from goin' next."

"Tiffy, I know. We need to do something because clearly she can't go on, but she has to. This is a big opportunity and we can't have her ass mess it up."

Tiffany agrees and walks back to the line. "Text me, girl."

Charm says okay and hurries to the car. With the key in the ignition, she comes violently out of her parking spot. She needs-for-speeds off into the street and looks for a gas station. Passing slow cars and swerving lanes to get by. Finding a Quick Mart on the side, she pulls into it with no ease. Her car pulls up and she parks it diagonal in the parking spot to where the car next to her can barely pull out. The people at the gas station feel her presence as soon as she skirts into the lot, causing a ruckus and scaring customers. She runs into the Quick Mart to the medicine aisle, searching for the best brand. With no time to look at the back label information, she picks up this carton called Dixie's and paces to the drink section to look for a ginger ale. Grabbing a small can, she takes it to the front and pays for her things, leaving without her change. Charm runs to her car and she sees that the other driver is waiting for her in fury. As she fusses a storm, Charm ignores it and gets in the car. The lady gets closer to Charm's window, tapping on it. Charm resists the urge to respond due to the matter that is at hand for her. She puts in her keys and drives off, whipping her caboose around and speed racing to the audition. She grabs her bag off the passenger seat after she pulls in and parks. Swinging the bag around her shoulder, she notices the cups that Sade had her drinks in. Charm picks one up and notices a green smudge at the bottom of the cup. The comments she made early about giving them lemonade intrigues her. She moves the cup up to her nose and sniffs, noticing it has a weird smell to it. Flipping back her switch to the issue of Sade, she darts out the car and runs back to the line. Tiffany and Sade are five spots away from being next. Tiffany shares a relief that Charm is back while Sade's antics are rubbing on the people behind her as she talks to the group behind them.

"I'm so sorry, y'all," Charm says to the dance group behind them, turning Sade back to her.

"Oh my Gooooood! Chaaaaaaaarm, I miss youuuuuu!" Sade yells, bear hugging Charm in a sloppy way.

"Tiffany! Open Sade's mouth wide while I pour this aspirin and this drink into her."

Tiffany makes an uncomfortable face with Charm's order. "You sure about this? We look like we're drugging her up in front of these people."

"Well, what do you want to do?! Have her embarrass us, knowing we let this happen or know we tried?"

Tiffany feels indifferent, understanding how much she wants this audition, but hesitant on the cost of Sade's health.

"Fine." Tiffany holds Sade down as she grabs her face and tells her to open. Charm opens the Dixy's carton and puts two in her mouth while pouring in the can of ginger ale.

"Swallow it all, Sade. Don't let any drip from your mouth." Sade gulps down every bit of the drink, freezing in her senses as she comes back to an upright position and her eyes look better in vision. Charm and Tiffany inspect her as if they were doctors, observing her behavior and noticing if there are any differences in Sade's behavior before the aspirin and after the aspirin. Charm uses her test theory and slightly pushes her shoulder to see her balance. Sade falls back, but it does not look too bad. Next, Charm tells her to look at a restaurant down the street and to give the name.

"It's Cub's Restaurant."

"Yes!" Charm says with enthusiasm, coming close to passing the test.

Tiffany thinks of another plan that requires more movement. Seeing how well she can move, she tells Sade to Michael Jackson spin-move on the spot.

"Ready, set, go."

Sade spins around smoothly, but hobbles off balance on her landing. "Damn!" Tiffany says, stomping her foot. The line moves closer to where they are two spots away 'til their turn. Charm scratches her hair, feeling the pressure for the group as Sade's behavior is the same.

"Okay look!" Charm says, huddling Tiffany and Sade together. "Sade, we are goin' to have you only do the last pattern to the song. In the meantime, Beyonce-pop it in the back except on transitions. Tiffany, we will execute most of the dance, but adjust our landmarks and coordinations due to how she will be in the back mostly."

"Got it!" Tiffany says. Sade doesn't say anything initially, but her true feelings flip a switch in her abnormal state. "Hell nawwwwww, Charm! I can do this. I'm okay."

"No, you can't!" Charm says with frustration.

"Yes, I cannnnnnn. You just don't want me to shiiiiiiine so you can dance next to him in the video."

Charm shakes her head with contention. "Sade, no! We are about to be up and you can barely land your moves on balance."

"It was just one move. You actin' like the choreo is just ONE MOOOOOVE!" Sade yells as the waiting line becomes quiet. Charm yanks her shirt and tells her to quiet down.

"Look! Tiffany, do you feel the same?" Charm says as Sade looks at her with disappointing puppy eyes and poked-out lips.

"Sade, we all know you the best in the group, but you not it today and we just need your role to come down a bit, so we can still have the dance and look on point."

Sade dismisses her comments and says, "That's bullshit." Charm and Tiffany see her disappointment, but move on with no remorse.

"So you got it?"

"Oh, I got it alright," Sade says with sarcasm out the side of her mouth. She watches Charm and Tiffany begin to stretch and get loose. Charm folds her arms near Sade, stretching her back. Tiffany bends over to stretch her legs in front of Sade's mid-section, stretching her groin. Sade stays in place with no stretch or movement. The group decision keeps her still. Stale-faced and tense in demeanor, she contains her fury. She goes out with the girls anyway. Setting places on stage, Tiffany and Charm assemble in the front as Sade aligns behind them in the middle, giving her less face time for the director to see.

"What is the name of this group?" the director says, bending forward his glasses to get a better view.

"S.T.C, sir!"

"Okay ladies. Ready when you are."

Tiffany and Charm bend their heads down in unison while Sade keeps her face upright with a look on her face, dripping her anger on the set. Eventually, Sade gets ready before they play the song.

Once the beat plays, Charm and Tiffany go to work, showcasing their moves out the gate. Bending knees, rocking hips more than the directors can handle. Beyonce popping with little pop for them to handle, Sade starts the dance with sincerity as she struts with each pop. A curly back that springs and coils to each beat. Then, it slows down in emphasis as the rest of the group looks more bootylicious than her. Charm dazzles with her moves, hyping Tiffany with each lean to the left and lean to the right, emphasizing each muscle flex to the boom of the bass and more unh to the melody of the song. Their feet patty cake around Sade in a circle two times as she continues to pop, making her back tired as she looks at the energy of her partners. Sade holds herself to break the fold, sweating more bullets than them to join in. The next move is the Michael Jackson spin move that Sade couldn't stick, boiling inside for that one move as her face turns red. After that part of the routine is the Scotch.

If it wasn't for me, they would've not learned the Scotch, she thinks, feeling the repetitive pops make her back tight. Charm smiles into the sky bright as she jigs and hops. Tiffany turns her swagger on, letting the judges see her moves as she hops and jigs. Together, it becomes a star-studded tandem shining bright to where every person at the director's table is amazed. Sade tries to make fearsome faces, hoping one of the judges can see a peak of her instead of her through the lead performance of her partners, but it doesn't work. The culminating hops and jigs lead to a groovy double Dutch that overshadows Sade completely. Sade and Tiffany transition to move to both sides of Charmin in the middle and swing imaginary ropes while she does the Scotch. Swaying her shoulders and rocking her hips, Charm handstands and jumps on one hand while flailing her body on beat in the middle. Switching with Tiffany, she jumps in, flipping her way to the top, hitting every landing with a Scotch jump, wowing the judges with her creativity and jumps that continue to deflate Sade's balloon ego. After a grandstand flip, Tiffany begins to jig and feel her way out of the ropes. Sade locks in with close attention as Tiffany begins to move out. Sade's impulse that was confined follows Tiffany as she is about to exit. All guards in her nerves try to stop this feeling as Sade watches Tiffany dance her way out. The exit of Tiffany's jump goes by in slow motion, as the impulses on Sade's left shoulder bounce and the little sister of her right shoulder wants to follow. Reacting off her untamed impulse, she two-steps into the ropes prematurely. She shows her fresh bunnies, hitting single flips, double flips while landing somewhat on a decent jump.

Charm and Tiffany's eyes widen, dumbfounded with shock to see her jumping in, but they go with the unscripted flow. Sade continues to go with her tongue out, throwing twisty-finger signs in the air as she comes down. Jumping back up in the air, Sade tries to flip three times. The first flip elevates to the sky. The second flip elevates to the moon. The third flip elevates to another galaxy, having her come back down with no control, landing awkwardly off balance and causing her to stumble sideways and fall on the ground. Like a fumbled mic', she lies there as if she dropped the moment. The song stops and Tiffany runs to help her up. Sade gets up slowly and then runs to the trash can off stage to throw up. Charm stands with hot red veins throbbing out of her head. A preheated statue, Charm is hot and speechless. Tiffany grabs Sade back to the stage and looks back at the director for any words.

Shaking his head, the director says, "Sorry, guys," and directs them to leave.

Sade looks at Charm with sorrow, but Charm walks off with silent apathy. No sense to help or deal with Sade. Sade runs to Charm, yelling, "I'm sorry. I'm sorry," but Charm ignores her and gives her the cold shoulder. Sade feels bad watching her walk off. Tiffany grabs Sade and escorts her off the stage away from a boiling Charm.

The drive home is soundless. Every gulp of swallowing saliva and clearing of throats speaks volumes in a car full of tension. Charm drives in cruise control, letting the tension marinate on Sade, constantly looking at her through the front-view mirror. Tiffany gazes out the window, finding awkward relief with the invisible car tunes as she rocks her head and bumps to the songs in her head.

Sade feels bad, showing a death sentence face as if she did a profane act. The weight on her shoulders keeps her down for the majority of the car ride home until she gets notifications on her phone, buzzing in her bag. She takes out her phone and looks at videos sent to her, finding reassurance and a soft smile when she gets dropped off at her house. Getting out of the car, she waves to the car with a little cheer, feeling better in her mood as she walks to her front door.

Charm drives off with a colder mood than the car A/C. Tiffany looks at Charm and stares at her sharply, knowing she feels the needle of her look poking her. Charm tries to look away, masking any relief to show empathy.

"Charm!" Tiffany says, grabbing her attention while she drives. "Why you so mad? So what she fell and threw up? She actually looked good before all that."

Charm gives a heartless face, murking at her comments. "Girl, are you serious?!!"

"Whatchu' mean, Charm?! Yeah, she fucked up, but it's over now."

"Nawww, Tiffy. It's the principle of how she fucked up!"

"Girl, I'm upset just like you, but what can we do?! They knew we were the shit until Sade's fall. If she didn't fall, I believe we would've made the list," Tiffany says with vigor.

Charm pulls up to Tiffany's house and stops in front of her driveway. "You don't understand, girl! We allowed her to be fine with lettin' her hot-headed ego ruin some of our breaks, but this one I can't! First of all, she's always late. Second, she always has an attitude, and third, she's always about her. All three showed up today, you feel me?! Plus, I think that lemonade is the reason why she showed up on one today."

"Girl, whatchu' talkin bout?"

"That drink she tried to give us. I checked it out when I came back and it had a green smudge in the cup. I think the lemonade was made of something else besides lemons."

Tiffany gets out of the car, dismissing all the distress from Charm's mouth. She turns around before she goes to her door.

"Girl, you ruthless. You actin' like you ain't fucked up before! Yeah, she got baggage, but so do you and she's our friend. I'mma need you to check yourself right now." Tiffany ends it off, storming out of Charm's car.

"Fuck that! You need to check yourself!" Charm yells in disdain, driving off in ugly fashion.

She keeps it cool, walking inside her house. Charmin is there as soon as she cracks open the door.

"Sissssssss! Did y'all make it?! Did y'all make it?!" she says, running to her with all smiles for the answer.

Charm keeps a cracked, mild-mannered face and says no in disappointment. Charmin comes down in excitement and is surprised, making a sour face to the taste of her answer.

"What happened?"

Charm looks at her in disappointment, shaking her head. "It's a long story, sis. It's a long story, but did you go over to apologize to Sonny?"

"Naw, I didn't go, but I can go right now," says Charmin in a soft manner.

"Yeah, go do that and I'll tell you about it when you come back."

"Fine, but where they live?" Charmin asks.

"You know where Old Man Williams' house is?"

"Yeah."

"It's basically the house to the left of it, closest to the clubhouse."

Charmin says a flat okay and walks out the house, feeling pitiful for her big sister. She walks over to his house step by step, feeling Charm's burden and what stuff to makeup for Sonny. Walking to his doorstep, she hears loud noises in the house. Random chants from guys yelling "What!" "You See Me!" and "Yeah nigga!" Discouraged whether she wants to follow through with this or not, she rings the doorbell timidly. The noise stops and loud footsteps come closer to the door. The door opens and it's Sonny, who begins to laugh at Charmin's presence before any interaction is established.

"You here for some lemonade since I can't sell it no more?" he says, chuckling.

"No."

Sonny smacks his teeth. "Psscht! Then whatchu' want? You fuckin' up my 2K." He twists his nappy curls in annoyance.

"Honestly, I was finna' apologize, but you know what, it's all good," she says, walking away in disgust.

"Good! Because nobody wants your sorry ass apology witcha' humpback ass joggin' around the neighborhood. Why don't you jog yo' ass on home," he laughs and cackles at her.

Charmin turns around and explodes. "Man, fuck you! Bitch-ass nigga!" Then she catches her temper, composing herself for the sake of Charm and the energy to walk home.

Sonny continues to laugh, closing his door. Street lights come on as the sun winds down. The neighborhood gets crazy closer to dark, but Charmin has all the ammo ready to unload if triggered. Ready to buck at anything if need be. Thinking of ways to pop off at Sunny the next time she sees him. She begins to walk and then notices the lights at Old Man Williams' are on. A suspicious scene that is unfamiliar and intriguing. She walks to his front door, putting her ear on it to hear any noises. Then she walks backward to see why the light is on. She gets on her tippy toes to try to see some window action, but she notices the window blinds rustling. After a long stare through the window, the porch light switches off and on in the blink of an eye, spooking Charmin to run off his yard in a hurry. Despite how Old Man Williams' house scares her, she goes home with Sonny's last words to her in mind.

"What's wrong with you?" Charm asks in confusion when she walks in.

"Nothing, sis. Just nothing," Charmin says with malice.

"Did you apologize to him?"

"Nope," she says with pride poking out of her lips, not caring if Charm disagrees or has any say so, but Charm looks at her in agreement.

The sisterly bond shares the animosity for any person in that household and because she understands, Charm doesn't say anything at all. She hugs Charm and walks upstairs to her room.

It's a perfect day in the neighborhood where the trees are whistling along the breeze and the sun's melanin is shining upon the sky. It's too hot to trot or play outside so kids are taking it easy on this day, chillin' inside playing the video games or tuned in to a Netflix movie. Because no parents are home yet, some children have the luxury to eat all the junk food that their parents bought the previous Sunday, tearing through the potato chips and munching most of the crackers before the end of the week. Other kids have to resort to slimy bologna sandwiches and crusty peanut butter sandwiches as options, leaving most of their bellies empty.

Luckily, Charm came home from work early to bring Charmin some food. Charmin enjoys her food, chillin' in her room as she listens to Beyonce, but it feels like something is missing. Charmin is full, but not satisfied. What do she and kids like her need on a beautiful yet scorching day where the temperature record is 101 degrees? The answer comes with a white van, cruising through the neighborhood in a magic school bus fashion. Highly decorated with respected badges labeled that can change a kid's mood like the push pop, the big Neapolitan sandwich, or some famous cartoon character gumball treat that can cool down any day of the summer. The jingle rings along loud through its truck speakers, posting at one spot due to the high traffic flowing through the neighborhood. The sing-a-long siren alerts kids with more excitement than hearing the afternoon intercom on the last day of school. The neighborhood kids flood out their houses to hurry to get some ice cream because for some neighborhoods, the ice cream man may come two times the whole summer.

"Ice cream!" Charmin yells in her bed. She runs downstairs to put on her shoes.

"Where you goin'?" Charm asks, waking up from her couch snooze.

"You can't hear that ice cream song goin' off right now?" Charm pauses to radio in on the ice cream song, but it doesn't tune in for her.

"Nope."

"Well maybe you need to get your ears checked. You tryna' come?"

Charm laughs, saying, "How you gonna jog this morning and eat ice cream in the same day?"

"Sis, don't do that," Charmin says with sass. "The ice cream man don't come that often, so you better get it when it's here. So you comin'?"

Charm smiles and gets up off the couch in agreement to put on her shoes. Charmin meets her at the door, ready to snag a cotton candy bar. Charm and Charmin walk out the house, watching as more people are walking in the direction of the sing-a-long. Charmin notices the wave, so she gets Charmin to follow the crowd. Heading in the direction, Charm finally begins to hear the jingle.

"Yo, how you heard this from our house?"

"I guess since you ain't a kid no more, it's hard to explain," Charmin says with her logic.

Seeing the white van with the big crowd around it, Charm and Charmin also notice Sonny is right next to it, selling lemonade from his stand. Charmin's face tenses up, recapturing the anger she felt yesterday in her mind. Next to it is Sade, jolly and happy to be promoting the business. Charm peeps her next to the stand and holds her angry water inside as she and her sister move closer to the ice cream man.

They wait in line to get ice cream. All kids are excited and horseplaying next to them as they wait. From the peripheral of Charm's eye, she notices Sonny talking and laughing with Sade as they boldly point in their direction. Charmin gets closer to Charm, whispering, "Yo, you see them over there?"

Charm leans into Charmin and says yes quietly.

"If they keep pointing over here, I might snap and go over there."

"Naw, don't do that, Charmin. We just here for the ice cream, not for the foolery."

Charmin nods with her in agreement and remains composed, flushing all animosity for the sake of ice cream. Charm and Charmin gets up to the order spot after the five people in front of them get their ice cream quick. Charm orders a bunny tracks cone while Charmin orders her cotton candy bar. Great options among the limitless treats they carry. They both receive in time as Charmin takes no time taking off the wrapper and licking the bar.

"Sis, this has to be the best one on that menu," Charmin says, enjoying her taste of the bar.

"Girl, this one is. Always been since I was a kid."

"See, you don't know flavor. Your tastebuds outdated or missing some flavor," says Charmin, laughing as they prepare to walk back. Out the blue, a little kid runs to Charmin from behind them and says, "Excuse me?"

"Hey, friend!" Charmin says with all smiles.

"The man over there told me to tell you to get your lemonade, humpback," he says with an innocent smile.

"He said what again?" She bends down to hear the child clearly.

"The man over there told me to tell you to get your lemonade, humpback."

"What was the last part?" Charmin asks for clarity.

"Oh, humpback." The kid laughs in her face and runs away, raising the thermometer of Charmin's cool past the boiling point.

"Oh hell naw," Charmin says, turning around and walking to the lemonade stand.

"Humpback? Why he call you humpback?" Charm grabs Charmin before she makes a move.

"Yesterday when I tried to apologize, this nigga was outright disrespectful from the jump. Laughing in my face, callin' me humpback, all of that, so I don't know about you, but he needs to be addressed," says Charmin with malice.

"Fine, but don't come off on some hot girl stuff. Be respectful first."

"Bet!" Charmin walks over to the lemonade stand, seeing prey in her eyes. Sonny smiles in her walk over to him, finding comedy in her attitude.

"Why, how are you today, ma'am?" Sonny greets her in vaudeville fashion.

"Nawww don't give me that," Charmin dismisses him. "If you got something to say to me, you say it to my face!"

"Oh, what are you talking about?" says Sonny in a dumbfounded way.

"That little kid you sent to me!"

"Oh, I just told him to tell you to come get some lemonade."

"No, you said more than that. Plus, you not even supposed to be sellin' lemonade."

"Oh yes I can, since yo' ass lied and got somebody to impersonate the association manager to tell me I can't. See, that's crazy, but it's all good because I see everybody doesn't want to see another black man succeed around here."

Stuck in her lies, she claps back. "Well, I wouldn't have to do that if you didn't take down our yard sale sign."

Sonny yells with all children around him. "Bitch, nobody took down your stupid yard sale sign!" The profane word echoes around the children near the ice cream truck and the lemonade stand, directing their attention to them.

"Oooooooooooo!" most of the little kids say, pointing at him whispering to each other. Sade walks over to Sonny with Charm walking over towards the scene, ready to disrupt.

"Yo, don't you ever call my sister that word again or me and you gonna have a problem!" Charm says with anger.

Sade walks in and pulls Sonny back to chime in. "Yo, watch how you talkin' to my brother. He ain't mean it."

"Well apparently he did if he gonna tell a kid to call her humpback too."

"Look, he don't mean it, so relax!" Sade says with a firm tone.

"So you gonna let him not apologize to my sister. Pschtt! Sounds like some shit y'all would do."

"Oh, just like you would allow your sister not to apologize after I came to you and told you what she did. Yeah, like you the one doing the right thing," Sade says with sarcasm.

"Well, I apologize for her actions, so how 'bout it?"

"He don't need to apologize because the root of all the mess begins with her when she shut down my brother's stand, so no." Sade's response fires up Charm in an aggressive way.

"But he called my sister a BITCH!" Charm yells.

"Well, it seems to me she was actin' like one the way she rolled up on him." Sade snickers, shattering the respect in the confrontation.

Charm explodes with a tick, grabbing both sides of the table and flipping Sonny's lemonade stand, knocking over all his juice on the ground as she steps up to Sade, knocking her on her back. The kids with ice cream gasp, walking over to see the mess.

"I can't believe yo' bitch ass!" Charm yells with hulkish fury.

Sade gets up from her hulk explosion and ensues to swing at Charm, grabbing hair and throwing punches. Charmin runs into the middle of the fight to break them up. Sonny jumps in and grabs on Charm's foot like a stand so Sade's momentum can knock Charm on the ground. Once Charmin sees what Sonny is trying to do, she comes at him in a carnivorous way, attacking him like a Tasmanian devil. Fists, elbows, knees, and shoes; a malice macarena in action as Charmin continues to beat him up. In the middle of the chaos, Charles' car speeds up to the side and parks mid street. Charles and Josh hop out and run to break up the fight. All the kids yell in excitement, phone-recording the footage of the madness. A movie scene in broad daylight. Charles runs to Charm's defense to drag her off of Sade as they cling on to each other's hair with massive grip. Josh runs in timidly, not knowing what to do, but grabbing Charmin as Sonny swings at her, knocking him in the head after finishing Charmin.

Charles sees Josh get knocked in the head and runs over like a bull that sees red. He grabs Sonny, picks him up, and throws him to the ground. Sonny lands on his front with no brace of the fall, tumbling to the ground. Charles checks on Josh and Charmin as Charm and Sade continue to duke it out. All of a sudden, a loud gunshot goes off, evacuating the scene as kids scatter in directions and the ice cream van pulls off. Charles grabs Charm while Josh drags Charmin to Charles's car and they drive off. Nobody knows who ringed off the gunshot, but the sound disperses the commotion.

The Aftermath

"Yo, what just happened?!" Charles yells to Charm and Charmin in the backseat as I remain my best strong from the fist that I received from Sonny.

"Man, that bitch called my sister a bitch," Charm says, fixing the messiness of her hair.

"Wait, what? I thought you and Sade were cool?" Charles asks in confusion.

"Fuck her, Charles. As for here on out, I don't want to ever hear that name ever in my life again."

"Ouuuuuuch. Well, you know that's not going to happen," Charmin says, laughing in a painful way.

Charles and I sit in the front, still taking in the turn of events that just took place. It's crazy how my brother picks me up off the street after I get done with my grass cutting, drive off, and about a block or two, we run into Charm and Charmin scrappin' for their lives across the street. I knew Charmin had a little edge since I first met her, but I never thought I would see her fighting in fruition. Charles and I help take care of their battle wounds. Well, mostly Charles takes care of their battle wounds. I just got the orders to get certain supplies and retrieve it to him. After the band-aid peelin' and ice bag coolin', we sit on the couch and get to the details of the situation.

"So for real though, Charm. How this all happen?"

"I would love to tell you what happened!" Charm says until Charmin cuts her off.

"Fuck that! All we were doin' was going to get some ice cream. When we got there, Sonny and Sade was posted next to the van, selling their lemonade, which was dumb as fuck because no kid is finna choose lemonade over ice cream," Charmin says with disgust. "Anyways, we got our ice cream and was about to leave until Sonny sent this little kid up to me, talkin' bout come get my lemonade, humpback. I heard him say humpback, but I didn't believe it to be true, so I asked the kid to repeat it again and he said the same thing, laughing and running off. So I got mad and me and Charm knew Sonny told the little kid to say that, so he needed to be addressed. We went over there. Words were said respectfully back and forth until he ended it off by calling me a bitch. Charm stepped in to try to defuse the situation with Sade and Sonny, but Sade basically agreed with Sonny calling me a bitch. Once she said that, all hell broke loose and here we are now," Charmin concludes.

Charles takes a deep sigh and tells me to go with Charmin to her room like they are about to have a grown folks talk. I walk with Charmin upstairs to her room not knowing how to handle this situation. Charmin flops on her bed with her eyes closed while I sit in her chair. I let her be because I don't know how she feels. What should I say? The nerve of this dude to call her that word. This man has been fishy ever since I first got his lemonade and now, I'm glad that my intuition is confirmed after today. It's funny because before today, I never been or jumped in a fight, but it's crazy how both Charles and I were ready to go in. Once I saw Sonny hittin' Charmin, an inner beast erupted, having me jump out the car first to lead the charge. Adrenaline rush and everything despite how I didn't know how to proceed. I just wish I would've come out the gate swingin' instead of trying to find my way into the fight. Next time, it will be different and I won't get hit, especially if they lay a hand on Charmin.

"You okay?"

Charmin rolls in her bed and gives me the eyes drawn with a rhetorical glare.

"I'm sorry. You've been a soldier all week, so I didn't know."

Charmin sits up in her bed. "Whatchu' mean?"

"Welllllll…" I scoot my chair towards her bed. "You the reason why we had a great yard sale. You got stung by a bee. You went to all these people's houses with no fear. I don't know. It just seems like you take punches, but always know how to keep it movin', ya know."

"Well, who says I'm down and out?" She points her question at me like I'm the answer.

"Nobody. I'm just sayin'."

"I gotcha," Charmin says with disheartenment. "So if you were me at the ice cream van, what would you have done?"

Ooooh, that's a tough one. "Ummm I don't know. I prolly would've got called a bitch and been like okay is that it?"

Charmin busts out laughing, holding her head to comfort the blows she took. She finishes her session and looks at me in a funny way. "Calling somebody a bitch is the worst thing you can call somebody, especially me. I don't even let people call me baby, but if you call me a bitch, then I have to kill you."

"I can understand that," I say.

"Look, I know you've never been in a fight or whatever, but there are some things you can't let people get away with, especially people like Sonny. It's people like him everywhere, ruling the world, walking the street, selling us lemonade." I giggle from her last remark. "It's up to us to stop the madness, ya know, or the world becomes impervious to bullshit."

I look at her, understanding her sentiment. Feeling the backbone in her voice when she said it too. Charmin always seems to have depth and understanding of any situation. Moving my eyes to her Ipod in the moment, I notice Beyonce's Formation song on pause. Intriguing to me after she just dropped her gem.

"I guess you were listening to Formation before you went out there to fight, huh?"

"Huh?" Charmin looks over to see what I see. "Maybe. That doesn't mean anything."

"Yeah it does," I say, chuckling. "It means you were really tryna' 'slay' on Sonny instead of beat on Sonny."

"Shut up, Josh. Please believe Beyonce is not gonna stop me from whoopin' somebody's ass."

"It might stop you from whoopin mines," I say on the sly. After my comment, she throws a pillow at my face, knocking me on the covers. As I'm on her bed, she puts her knee on my chest and looks down on me. "We friends and all, but I can still beat you up," she says, smiling over me in a threatening way. Looking up at her, I want to disagree, but I was okay with her way this one time. Charm walks in the room unexpectedly to see what she sees.

"Ummm, Charmin, it's Magic. He wants to speak to you," she says with a phone in her hand.

"Okay. Let me talk to him privately in my room, Josh," I agree, coming from underneath her to go downstairs to sit with Charles. Charm's eyes escort me out the room with a questionable look. It's funny how Charles looks beat even though he was doing most of the beating. Just the view of him flying Sonny off of me just like I did Charmin's dog when he tried to come after me. The military combat must have set in when he saw me helpless in the fight.

Five minutes later, Charmin comes down to tell us what Magic said.

"What he say?" Charm ask.

"So basically, he got word and got footage that I started the brawl. We kept goin' back and forth about the story he heard and the story I told him, but he had the last say."

"Why didn't you tell him to talk to me?" Charm says. "I could have gotten everything straightened out."

"I guess I didn't want it to affect everybody else. Due to the footage and rumors that he received about me starting the fight, I can't volunteer with the kids at the clubhouse no more."

Charm goes to her for comfort, knowing how special the children are to her. I feel bad too because I know she wants to do something nice for them. All the kids love to be around her like a big sister.

"Wait. It was just you and Zoe. Now that you are gone, they're gonna have to find somebody quick or them kids will run over Zoe," Charm says.

"Well, I gave them a recommendation of somebody," she says as she swings her eyes my way. Hoping she is talking about Charles next to me, I begin to feel that she is not.

"Who did you recommend?" Charles asks.

"Josh."

Charles starts laughing. "Bwahahahaha. Josh?! What makes you think Josh can look after them kids?"

"I just have a good feeling about Josh and I know he won't let me down. Plus, it will be mostly in the afternoons, so it doesn't interfere with your grass-cutting business as well."

"Well, what do you think, Josh?" Charles asks.

I look at him and then I look at Charmin in an unresponsive way. The information is pretty new to me to where I can't believe she recommended me. I haven't been with a child since taking care of my little cousin the other year and that barely went well. Due to my lack of experience, I didn't know if I should take this on or not. Children can wear you out, especially the bad ones. I try to take care of myself, but how can I try to take care of children? Charmin looks at me in an awkward way, wanting me to say an answer. The thought of taking care of children makes me feel like I got a baby on the way. Shotgun wedding next in line as well. Honeymoon vacation at the neighborhood pool with Uncle Charles and Aunt Charm helping me along the way. It's all downhill from there.

"Josh!" Charles says to get my attention.

"Huh?" I say, coming out of the daydream of my future family with the children. I know I can do it since it's only in the afternoons. The motivation to do it is for Charmin, so she can get back clean with her reputation.

"Are you going to do it?" Charmin asks.

"Yeah, I'll do it," I say with little care. "When do I start?"

"Tomorrow at 1. Just go in there and help Zoe for a few hours and then you are fine."

I look at Charmin with my best happy-to-help smile, but a part of me is antsy about doing it. Charles and I stay for a little more time to comfort and care and then we leave to go back home. Worn out from the day, Charles and I go to our separate rooms and go to sleep. He and Vickie have finalized what they want to do for the mural and tomorrow morning they will begin to work on it. I have a couple lawns to cut before going to the clubhouse tomorrow, so I know tomorrow will be a day of days.

●••••••••••••••••••••••●••••••••••••••••●

My alarm goes off before my body rooster wakes me up. A mix between the night and morning in the sky, I wake up with little effervescence about the day. The adrenaline from the fight has worn off to where I feel the real aftermath of it today. Sore spots in my shoulders and chest, making it hard to stretch my arms. I struggle with my routine as I zombie walk each trip from the bathroom to my room, forgetting to brush teeth or wash my face. All I want to do is put on a shirt, grab my banana as my lunch pail, and go to work. I go to my first house, just scanning the amount of green grass that can take up a front yard. The front yard is like the house owner's head; he doesn't have a big head, but the hair on it is thick. If my lawn mower had some adjustable clippers, I wouldn't be so worried. I start off cutting the grass with ease, talking to the grass. Being one with the grass. Because it's early in the morning, the grass is dewy, feeling all the grease in this hair and he didn't put on a durag. Nonetheless, I take my time, cutting the grass. Making my way around his garden and getting the small spots around his mailbox. The task takes me up to about an hour. I go back to him with my hand out, ready to get the money, and he hands me $10.

"Excuse me sir, but you owe me ten more dollars. Your lawn was not easy to cut, especially with the weeds in the front," I say with a Charmin assertion. The days of getting screwed are over as I don't leave. The man looks out the door and agrees to the job well done and gives me the ten I ask. I walk off his doorstep, patting myself on the back and say goodbye to the lawn.

Oooo that lawn looking good with his fresh cut I just did. All the water sprinklers gonna be on him now.

A wizard with the lawn mower. I strut my way to the next house for the day as the sun is out, making me come alive from the slow morning. Coming up the hill, I see another sign, hoping that it isn't what I think it is. But it is. Sonny's lemonade stand again, ruining my beautiful mood after I got paid with a bonus. How is Charmin facing consequences and he's not? Questions that need answers the next time I see Charmin. He sees me and looks through me, raising the heat index of the tension in my walk. Ignoring the glare, I just continue to walk while my heart beats as if I'm on a tightrope to the next house. A little kid runs up with his basketball to get some lemonade, removing the tension in the air and the hostile look from me. I just cruise on by with my lawn mower, wishing karma can serve him.

I come to my second house, making me second-guess whether I want to do it because of the shape of the lawn's head. With the last one, the lawn was flat and easy to maneuver, but this one has a curvy head with slopes. For the first time this summer, I have a lawn on a hill. All this walking and more leg action to go. I come to the door and let the lady know that I'm here, which surprises me that the lady is handicapped, living on a hill. I start on the bottom of the hill and take my laps, working back and forth. Leg drive and kick slide, leg drive and kick slide. Either way, my legs are done after each lap. It takes me about two hours to get done due to my lack of endurance during the cut. I had to take breaks in between to let my legs cool down before they cramp again. Once I'm done, my legs are all around sore. The lady is impressed with my cutting skills to where she gives me twenty-five dollars. Thank God for the tip. At least, I know that leg catastrophe wasn't for nothing. I get so happy to where I hurry back to the house to save the bonuses and eat the saved sandwich that Charles had waiting for dinner. "He will be okay" as I leave ten dollars on his bed with a note that says "Go treat yourself."

I go take a shower and put on some more clothes, knowing the children would not want to smell grass when I come in the clubhouse. Charmin texts me as soon as I get ready to walk over there, just to make sure I don't forget. I let her know that I got it and I am on my way to the clubhouse. Walking in, I see Zoe playing Uno with four little girls in a circle. Instead of saying hello once I came in, she is focused on her hand. A serious demeanor on every player in the circle. Poker faces with their cards pushed to their shirts to where they can only see them. One of the girls jigsaws through her hand of cards to throw down once cards are played. She figures it out and throws it down. Next, Zoe has the spotlight with the smallest amount of cards. The battle is between her, who has two cards left, and this girl with pigtail braids, who has one card left. After everyone goes, Zoe puts down her draw four card for another girl and changes the color to blue.

"Uno!" Zoe says. Then she slams her last blue card on the ground. "Uno Out! Hah-hahahaha!" Zoe gloats in front of the girls. The joy of the girls' spirits comes down as Zoe continues to show off. Getting up, she comes over to acknowledge me.

"Hey, you're Josh, right?"

"Yeah."

"Nice to meet you. My name is Zoe." We shake hands. "So this is like the neighborhood daycare. As you can see, it's very hard to manage everybody." Hinting at the boys, who begin to roughhouse with Lego blocks and cars. "But you come at a good time. You come right when they eat their lunch, then they watch a movie or nap, and then we play with them for a while, and then their parents pick them up."

"Okay cool," I say as she simplifies the routine every day.

"So I'mma have the girls and you will have the boys. As a matter of fact, CLASS!" She yells to grab the kids' attention. All the kids stop what they're doing and look at her in synchronization. "Everybody come circle up in Five!" All kids scramble to get to her. "Four!" Straightening the circle and their posture so it's not a raggedy oval. "Three!" All kids fix their criss-cross applesauce. "Two and One!" All eyes on us.

"Everybody, I would like for you to meet your new teacher, Josh. Everybody says hey Josh!"

"Hey Josh!!" all the kids repeat, smiling and waving at me. I wave back to them as they look so cute in their criss-cross apple sauces.

"Boys! He will be with y'all mostly, okay?"

The boys look at me and nod in agreement, trying hard to sit still and pay attention.

"It's lunch time, everybody. Go grab your lunch and let's eat."

All the kids say yaye and run over to grab their lunch bags. All the princesses have their Ariel, Jasmine, and Tiana lunch bags, ready to open up and eat their food. Conversations about what movie the class should watch over crackers and cookies. Cutie gossip about TV shows and clothes and sometimes boys. The girls bother Zoe during her break, asking her if they can watch such-n-such or what is the movie, but her lips are zip-lock sealed.

The boys, the fellas, all of them grab their solid color lunch bags. No decorations on it at all unless it's a speed racer and sit next to the girls. It's funny because the girls are nicely neat as they sit and eat their food while the guys are hanging off the chairs. One little man sits up down, eating out of his Doritos bag. Another boy is wasting cookie crumbs on the floor, making me laugh as I watch them. Then, another one is chillin' by himself with no food in his hand with an empty drinking cup. I feel bad as I notice everyone enjoying lunch time but him. Feeling concerned, I walk over to him and say wassup.

"Hey, how ya doin'?"

The little boy looks at me with a reserved face. The same face I made as a kid when a stranger talked to me.

"My name is Josh. What is your name?" I say with a smile.

"Rayland."

"How old are you, Rayland?" He puts up seven fingers. Like a teacher, I count all seven. "One, two, three, four, five, six, seven." He side smirks, glad to know that I can count.

"So why are you over here by yourself?" I ask with concern.

"Because I don't have no food."

"Well, why don't you have no food?"

"Because we don't have no food at home," Rayland says with shame. It's only my first day, but I already want to throw a field trip just so we can go to the McDonalds down the street and give him some food.

"Well, did you try asking them for food?" I point to the other boys eating. Rayland shakes his head no and tilts his head down in embarrassment. It hurts me to see him like this, so I lift him up and tell him to come with me. We go to the boys and girls to ask them for the food they don't want. Most of the boys say no or only give away their fruit. Walking through the girls' lunch corner, the girls are nicer to where you have some giving away some crackers and maybe one cookie. Another girl gives three fruit snack gummies. To me, that means a lot, but it doesn't change his mood as much. Once we accumulated all the scrapings from the other kids, it looks enough to equate a full snack meal. Rayland cheers up a little and begins to eat the fruit gummies and fruit while sipping the little drippings out of his cup.

"What's in the cup?"

"Lemonade."

"Where you get that from?" I ask.

"Sonny!" he says with a little spark. I notice his spark and it makes me wonder why he has a spark over him.

"How do you know Sonny?"

Rayland slowly delivers his speech and says, "From his lemonade stand."

"Did he talk to you or something?" I'm interrogating him like Sonny is a criminal.

"Yeah. We're friends," says Rayland as he bites his apple.

"How did y'all become friends?"

Rayland thinks about it. "He talks to me and he gives me free lemonade."

"Okay, okay cool." I say, finding peculiarity in the situation.

I sit with Rayland until he's done. He and the rest of the class get ready to watch their movie. Zoe turns on the TV and puts on a Netflix Disney movie called Moana. The girls hooray once they hear the opening movie song and see the credits. The boys begin to slouch, drooping their eyes as one scene transitions to the next. Five minutes later, the boys are down for the count except for Rayland wide awake as he sits next to me. I begin to lay down like the boys, doing my best to remain awake, but the movie knocks me out cold.

Zoe wakes me up toward the tail end of the movie, so I can remain attentive before the lights turn back on. After the movie, the girls get up to play tag and I play soccer with Rayland. He begins to show more expression toward the latter part of the day, giggling and laughing. A better mood you can say. Once parents begin to pick his classmates up, he comes back down. Rayland still remains at the center after six, so Zoe tells me that she will walk him home. I look at her and Rayland looks at her, wondering if I can walk him home. Googly eyes and all as I give her the look and he says please please please pretty please can Josh take me home? She laughs and says okay. Rayland jumps with joy and grabs his bag.

"Good to know you made a friend today," Zoe says with admiration.

Rayland and I walk together out of the clubhouse. On the way out, we see Charles and Vickie working on the mural. Vickie is spray painting one side and Charles is painting another side. The outline is not drawn; yet I like it. Rayland looks at them on the way with the same attention. Two masters crafting together a piece that I can ride and see every day I leave the house. Getting closer up the hill, Rayland runs.

"Rayland! Rayland!" He makes me run to catch up, but he keeps going.

"Sonny! Sonny!" he yells. Once he says that name, I begin to slow down. Taking my time to cross the threshold, I see Sonny at his stand, smiling in Rayland's face. Little does he know about his friend.

"Sonny! Sonny! I want you to meet my new teacher, Josh."

Sonny looks at me with a fake smile as I walk up. "Wassup."

I give him a mean head nod with a straight face. Scared on the inside, but thuggin' on the outside. It's funny because I never thought I would have a thug side to myself, but with the help of Charmin and Sonny, it's coming out.

"He gave me food and played with me too, Sonny," Rayland says.

"Oh that's sweet." Sonny picks up his cup and sips.

Clearing his throat afterwards, Sonny says, "Look, Rayland. It's getting late. It might be time for you and your friend to head home."

"No, it's not," Rayland says, puzzled.

"Look, Rayland, I'll talk to you tomorrow. Just get home safe." Sonny raises up and draws Rayland back to me. Rayland notices the Western gun draw stances Sonny and I have, ready to shoot if he moves or talks. Instead, we keep walking with no trouble. The walk back to his house starts silent, but then he says something to ice the mood.

"Do y'all know each other?"

I look at him, wondering what to say and how to put it. "No, but I know who he is."

"What do you mean??" Rayland asks.

Debating whether to sugar-coat or be frank, I say in a respectful way, "He's not a nice person."

"Why you say that?"

"He is mean to me and most of my friends."

"Why he do that?"

"I don't know. Maybe he was born that way," I say, playing with my fingers as I think about it.

"Nuh huh. He's nice to me and everybody I know. You sure you don't have him mixed up with somebody else?" Rayland says as we get to his house. So innocent and unaware of the situation.

"Yeah I'm sure," I say in a dry tone. "I'm glad we had fun today. I'll see you tomorrow."

"Okay. Bye, Josh," he says, waving at me as he runs inside.

As I walk back, I think about Sonny and his influence on kids like Rayland. I didn't know what to expect from the fountain of youth, but it's funny how they teach me things on what's going on and how they perceive it. It seems like before this summer, I probably thought the same as them. This summer is different, as meeting kids like Rayland reminds me of me, except he's seven years old.

●·················●·················●

"One! Two!"

("Run, Raylan Run!")

"Three! Four!"

("Where you goin', bro?!")

"Five! Six!"

("That way, that way!")

"Seven! Eight!"

("Hurry up!")

"Nine! Ten!"

("Shhhhhhhsh")

"Ready or not! Here I come!" I scream, turning away from base.

If life was a street game, it would be hide-and-seek. Could it be manhunt? Could it be cops and robbers? Most definitely, but it seems like the world is full of people that hide from the truth and then there are people that seek the truth. I used to hide from it, but now I seek it, searching every tube playground slide at a time.

"Gotcha!"

"Dangit!" Some of the girls are surprised that I found them so fast as they slide down one by one to go to base.

I look around the playground, but nothing else seems to trigger a hiding spot to me. Now I see trees that are wide and thick for a small child to hide for some minutes. It seems obvious for a spot to hide, but I know I would've hid there as a kid. Light footsteps as I creep behind the trees. Nothing in sight when I look around, but then something tells me to look up.

"Gotcha!"

The thing about little kids is that there will always be a few in the group that know how to climb trees.

"Awww man!" Four of the boys groan, making their way down off the branches.

"Be careful, guys!" I stay there to help them jump down. Heavy dudes as I catch some of them off balance.

I look some more, needing two more on my wanted list before I win the game. Nobody is behind the bushes as I double check. The wooded area next door is clear. Where are Rayland and Briana?

Oh yeah, I think I forgot the parking lot. Small, but could be a spot. I walk over to the parking lot and there's only one car parked there. A nice, big SUV for any kid to hide behind. I walk over to it and look underneath the car: First, for any culprits. Second, for any feet and it looks like to me that I see some feet. One pair of colorful Nikes and a pair of white Reeboks, just moving back and forth. Walking slowly to the other side of the car, I go along with the sound of the air, moving slow until a big sound pops up like birds chirping or a drive-by car. Tilting my head first, Rayland and Briana take off, sprinting together. Bonnie and Clyde on the run as they hold each other's hand. I go around to try to beat them. As soon as they see base, all the kids are cheering and screaming for them to make it.

"Hurry, hurry!" "C'mon!" "Run y'all run!"

Coming close to the base with me on their tail. I catch up with my longer strides to catch them in arm distance. Rayland and Briana jump to base with all their might.

"Safe! Safe! Safe!" they yell as the other kids cheer them on. I look at them, gasping for air. They smile in unison sparkle while huffing and puffing for air. I would argue, but I just knew I needed something to drink. Magic comes from behind me, laughing at my tiredness.

"I see you have your work cut out."

I just smile and try to stand back up.

"Hey kids, who wants lemonade?"

"I do! I do! I do!" "Me, me, me!" They raise their hands and sing for the glory of lemonade.

"Great! Sonny's Lemonade stand is around the corner. Josh will take you."

"Yayyye!"

I cut Magic off before he turns back. "Sonny's? Why we goin' to him? You didn't see the video?"

"Yes I did. And I saw him just like I saw you," he says, looking at me with audacity.

He shuts me right up even though there is more I want to say.

"Once I got the story, Sonny didn't start it. It was Charmin."

"But sir?"

Magic cuts me off. "Look, Josh. Sonny has been doing good lately; plus, his lemonade is real good. Also, we promote black businesses around here, especially our own." He lifts his fist before walking off. I gather the kids and have them walk in a single file line to Sonny. The animosity continues between me and Sonny as I walk up, but I am thirsty for his lemonade after that game. The kids line up in front of his stand. Each kid including Rayland has a dollar for a cup. I wait in the back of the line, hoping to get my cup on the sly so it doesn't look like I support him. As the line shortens, Briana comes from behind and walks up behind Crissy, her friend in line. Rayland is behind Crissy and looks at Briana in an impertinent way.

"Move, Bri, you can't skip."

Briana gives him the mean face. "Nobody is skipping, Rayland. Crissy saved my spot."

"That's still skipping."

"No, it's not."

"Yes it is."

"No it's not."

"Yes it is." Rayland becomes frustrated, trying to push Briana out of place, but she holds her ground.

"No it's not." Briana squares up on him and she's taller.

Rayland shrivels as his face tenses up in anger. "Bitch! Move!" Every kid's eyes inflate with astonishment. A word so foreign to the kid's language, but a word they know not to say.

After Rayland blows up in her face, Briana's face crinkles in an emotional way, running to the clubhouse as she holds back her tears. Crissy runs over to help her. Meanwhile, Sonny points at Rayland, saluting him for his disrespectful prowess.

"I see you, boy." He looks like a proud dad.

Rayland smiles and salutes him back like brothers. I was already in shock once Rayland said what he said, but once I saw Sonny congratulate the foolishness, I knew I had to do something.

"That's it. Everybody go back to the clubhouse."

"Awww man! Whyyyyyyyy?" the kids say.

"I SAID go back to the classroom, y'all!" The children get the message and scram back to the classroom as Magic walks out. I walk up to Sonny with so much rage.

"You need to leave!" He hears the bass, the treble, and the trouble in my voice, causing him to come forward.

"Says who, little nigga?" he whispers.

"Says me."

Sonny squares up, eye to eye, nose to nose. "And if I don't?"

"Hey, hey, hey, hey!" Magic comes up, pullin me back. "What's goin' on over here?"

"This man congratulated Rayland for calling Briana a bitch."

Laughing it off, "Man, c'mon. You gonna believe him?!"

"Is this true?" Magic says with sincerity.

"C'mon, Magic, it's me." He continues to laugh and brush it off. Magic looks at me and he sees the seriousness in my eyes.

"Sonny, I'mma need you to leave."

Sonny chokes on his laugh and heats up. "Are you serious? You gonna believe him?!"

"Sonny, leave!"

Sonny breaks down his lemonade stand sign and packs his stuff, staring at me as he breaks down each set. Once he is done, he looks at me with affliction and says, "I'll remember this," walking slowly away from the premises.

Magic walks me back to the clubhouse as I try to calm down my rage. So much more I saw happening in that moment for me and Sonny, which Magic stopped by stepping in. I go through the day thinking about the situation of Sonny and his effect on the kids. When I was watching the movie of the day, I couldn't fall asleep because The Joker in Batman made me think of Sonny and all I wanted to do was beat him to a pulp. So much restraint that day. Plus, I made Rayland apologize to Briana after the incident. He did it, but it seems like the connection between him and Sonny is too close to where this incident won't stop the two from being around each other. Once the day goes by, I decide to walk Rayland back to his house. Rayland hesitates coming with me to leave. My body language shows all my anger oozing out of my pores, but I knew I had to stay the "bigger person." Something Charles would say all the time. The disappointment toward Rayland remains, but I know he will do better. We walk out the clubhouse and stop near Charles and Vickie working on the mural. The way Charles and Vickie work calms me to take my mind off the situation a little. Charles is on the top of his ladder boldening the lines on the wall with his paintbrush. Vickie hangs on her ladder, leaning to the left with a ballet heel toe balance, showing him the small-scale map design of the mural. Charles with his art bifocals looks back and forth to straighten, to trim, to get everything to detail. I just have to stay and watch for a second. Rayland looks at me and asks, "Can I go get Zoe to walk me back?"

I look at him in an appalled way, thinking of all the things to say, he says that.

"Sure," I say with little care in the world. One day, I can put him on to the striking wonder that is art. Magic walks up to me and watches them with me.

"I'm sorry about today."

I look at him with no expression. The statement of him saying sorry didn't do justice for me.

"Why are you sorry? You didn't do anything."

"Well, if I didn't have the kids get lemonade from him, this probably would have never happened."

"Yes it would. Being around Rayland shows me how kids like him and many others want to be like Sonny in the neighborhood."

Magic smiles and says, "That's why it's good to have you around to help keep them on a straight track, so they don't follow down the behavior. Then again, Sonny is not a bad kid. He just needs somebody to stay on him."

"Was it like that when you grew up here?"

"Of course. Some things are not new under the sun. It's just different. The neighborhood had its bad bunch of kids, but most kids were good. It seems like kids get more in to trouble nowadays doing stupid stuff. And once one kid does something bad, it just becomes an outbreak around here."

I look at him and see the disheartment on his face as he reminisces. He continues to go on about the complaints he receives about the neighborhood kids and the crimes and how some people don't want to move in because of the mess. Looking at the mural, he hopes their masterpiece can revitalize a good image that once was associated with the neighborhood. A positive beacon on the wall that can be a light and show prominence for the kids and homeowners.

"Yeah the mural is nice, but that isn't going to do promises. You need to do something else," I say.

"I will. Just have to think about it."

I look at Magic and let his last line settle, passing through ideas of what is that something the neighborhood needs. Then I think about Charmin and her telling me about the legend of Old Man Williams. The legend helps me to think about the good ol' days of the neighborhood. A Mr. Rogers-type of neighborhood where people were nice and could get together. Wait a minute! "Get together." The neighborhood clubhouse party! That's what we need.

"Magic, why don't we bring back the clubhouse party?"

Magic questions it. "Seeeeeeee. I don't know if the neighborhood can handle that."

"Why not?" I say on the contrary. "We need something like this to show why the neighborhood is not a bad place and remind people why we should not trash it. So many things you are doing for the neighborhood and this should be a celebration for it."

Magic shakes his head. "I don't disagree with you, but I don't know if kids will like that. Doing clubhouse parties was a thing for my day. I don't know if y'all would be accepting of that."

"We would, Magic. We can probably put a spin on it, say like do it on the same day the mural is ready to be shown to the world and we can celebrate."

"That's actually not a bad idea, Josh."

"So let's do it."

"Hold your horses now," says Magic, thinking about it. "It's a lot of planning to do something like this. You have to get food, equipment, chairs, a DJ."

"Well, some things I know we can get for free and still have a good time."

Magic looks at me with juxtaposition. "So you know how to plan and can do all of this with a small budget?"

"Not necessarily, but I know Charmin can do all of this and would love to do this task. When it comes to planning, she knows how to get it done." I'm smiling as I think about the work ethic of my crush.

"Hmmmm." Magic hums, scratching his chin and looking at me. I give him a secure look, knowing he can trust me if he gets me the approval. The first thing I am confident and sure of all summer. All I need to do is get with Charmin and we can make this happen.

"So what do you say?" I look at him with my hand out, ready to shake.

Giving a heavy sigh, he wipes his face and sticks out his hand to grab mine. "Don't make me regret this."

"No problem, sir!" I'm ecstatic as I think about it and can't wait to tell Charmin, knowing she will love me for this.

"I will give you more details on it tomorrow."

I run back home, ready to eat dinner and take a shower as my day's highs and lows have me tired. Sinking into my bed, I get ready to take out my phone. Dialing her number puts a spell on me as my eyes begin to close and my body begins to shut down. The phone rings and picks up to where I hear her say hello, but my deep doze off leaves her no answer.

The Setup

"See? This the type of thing I wanted us to do," says Charmin with passion.

"Yeah," I say. "It's just that we have to plan fast and get everything set up."

"That's not a problem. What is the date he told us to have it?"

"He actually thinks the 4th of July would be a good day to have the occasion. So many people will be out and everybody in the neighborhood is going to try to pop fireworks. It's only right."

"Okay, cool. How's the mural coming along?"

I think about it as the piece is beginning to turn into a movie poster on a wall. I just wonder what they are doing with it. "It's beginning to look good. You can tell they are taking their time with the mural and giving it extra thought."

"Like what do you mean?" Charmin asks.

"It's how he always does with his paintings in which it's something deep, but it looks like Vickie is throwing in her vision to not make the mural too abstract, so the neighborhood can understand the message."

"Okay, cool. So here's the plan. Most likely, Magic is gonna have us stick with the 4th of July because of the festive spirit and everybody is goin' to do something to celebrate. So we can check that off."

"Check," I say as I listen to Charmin fire off her logic.

"Next, I will have you do the grassroots work of putting up flyers and letting people know word of mouth while I spread it on social media, putting it out on all pages and letting people know to put it on their pages."

"Okay. When do you think you can give me the flyers?" I ask.

"Honestly, I think I can give it to you tomorrow. You can just come and get it after being at the clubhouse."

"Okay bet."

"Cool. Thirdly, there's so much talent in this neighborhood where you have people doing different things, so different events have to take place for the kids and the people to be a part of when they come."

"What things you thinkin'?"

Charmin grabs her a piece of paper and pencil and begins to jot down. "We can get Vickie to do her Drink My Paint nonprofit with the people."

"But what if she is too busy with the mural and won't have time to do that?"

"Oh yeah, you right. We don't want to add more to her plate as she is already wrapped up with that," Charmin says, scratching that off the list.

"Ooooh," I say with a pop. "One time I went to a carnival and they had people, who would draw you as a cartoon. What if we had those people at the party? Those people who can draw them with the background of the mural? If people ask, he doesn't have to say nothing and once the mural is revealed, then it will make people happy that they got the mural added to their drawing."

"Now, that's a good idea, but that would take even longer to do for the caricaturist as the people wait. Look, I'll find a person who can conduct a sip 'n' paint for the party, to where it's no alcohol and kids from 1 to 92 can participate," Charmin says, writing it down. I look at her and say okay boss, finding joy in planning ideas.

"Okay what else?" Charmin thinks.

"Hmmm. How about a spoken word session inside one of the rooms of the clubhouse, where kids and anybody can go to an open mic and speak about what the 4th of July and this neighborhood means to them?"

"Now, I like that. Who are you goin' to let be over that?" Looking at her as if I'm the answer, smiling and what not.

"I don't know, but it's not you. You are going to walk around and make sure everything is good. Magic made you over this, not me," she says.

I see her point, giving her the touche. I wish I could help with the spoken word. I never had many interests in life, but spoken word looks cool to me. Breaking down the world into your law and preaching your speech with a figure of speech, while a cool cat in the back drums for the effects and my Oakley shades iluminates from the spotlight. Then after my set, all finger snaps applaud me and Charmin is right there when I walk off the set to say, "Oh my God."

"Josh!"

"Huh?" I say, snapping back to reality.

"You understand why you can't do so?"

"Yeah I do."

After she finishes writing the spoken word idea down, she says, "Okay. Any other ideas you think?"

I think about it and then mention how Charm is a dancer, feeling that she and the group can do a performance or something.

"Oh that's a great idea. We just need a DJ for them and they can perform. Thing is, I don't know how Charm is going to feel about performing since she and Sade are not on good terms."

"Maybe you can fill in?" I say with sarcasm. My comment ignites a silent flame from the sly smirk she gives me and begins to write the dance idea.

"Wait, are you serious? You gonna fill in?"

"Why not?" Charmin says. "I'mma make sure Charm lets me do it and then the rest will be history."

"What about the DJ?" I ask with wonder. "And oh yeah. Make sure kids are playing on the basketball courts too. Maybe a five-on-five competition."

Charmin jots my suggestion down. "Charm and the group is sort of cool with the people at the skating rink. If I can get her to put us on with the Friday night DJ, then we are going to be fine," she says, jotting a note next to the dance idea.

"Okay okay," I say, loving her plan. "So what about food and drinks?"

"Ask Magic for a good catering business to do the food and drinks and tell him the rest is in our hands. Plus, all the events Magic throws from time to time, I know he got more connections to make it come alive."

"You right. Okay I'll let him know tomorrow."

"Cool, and I'll come by tomorrow to let him know the plan before we start putting the word out."

"Great!" I say, feeling the joy and anticipation of this party. I never did nor planned anything of this magnitude and now I have a chance to let this party impact the neighborhood.

Charmin smiles in a proud way as she comes over to walk me out of her house. Before I leave the doorstep, she says, "Hey. Thanks again for letting me plan this with you. This really means a lot and for the children at the clubhouse."

"No problem. I just knew I had to include you." I twinkle with my smile, so she feels the effect as I smile hard in my head.

Charmin comes over and gives me a hug with her Huggies soft baby skin. I squeeze her and I feel the summer breeze on her shoulders when I put my head across it. Letting go, she says goodbye and I float my way back home, holding on to her summer breeze until I get to my bed. Most nights, I change into my night clothes for bedtime, but I want to keep the feel and keep the scent that laminates on me from Charmin. I can't wait for the party.

Finally, a day off. Bossman Charmin had me running flyer routes as I do my lawn care routes in the morning. Clocking in and clocking out as I do steel-mill shifts to help the clubhouse party come to fruition. Blowing steam from sunup to sundown for the neighborhood. Every day, I continue to tell the kids about the party and have them pass out flyers when they go home. I get paid in happiness. They get paid in Smarties that I get from the store as an incentive to them. Sometimes, Airheads when they do a good job. The kids never run out of energy when I come in at noon. Their ATP increases due to the fact that they get tired of Zoe by the afternoon; well, at least the boys. Then they play with me until I'm down and out. Dodgeball, tag, sometimes Monopoly or Spades. One of the little kids almost cussed me out because I reneged and we lost the game. We were cool a few days later. Also, Rayland continues to be my main man, but his connection with Sonny is strong. It's like he gets the best of both worlds. One day, he's thuggin' and then he's nice on another day.

I try to be a good role model despite the circumstances. Rayland needs to know more about Sonny's life than what Sonny shows him. Once the kids go home, I continue to check in on Charles and Vickie as the mural is coming together. The tarp stays on while they work so people don't see them in action, but I sneak in to watch them. Charles comes back every day happy and fulfilled when I see him at the house. The dream he never could've imagined. I'm glad the mural is helping him earn some change and live his dream. Meanwhile, Magic is giving us the platform for the party to be great. Lending us his connections and letting Charmin sit in his office to call all the contacts in his book. She puts the party on his social media pages, planning to make this party the biggest thing since sliced bread.

In her spare time, she practices with Charm and Tiffany for the performance. She's been telling me how she can dance so well that it hypes me up to see her move. Overall, the neighborhood is ready for the big dance on the Fourth. As I lie here in my bed and do nothing all day, I think about the party and what I may do afterwards.

Briing! Briing! Briiing!

I open my eyes in disapproval. Where did I put my phone?

Briing! Briing! Briiing!

I continue to look for it, rustling through my pillow and covers as the turmoil makes it flip on the floor. I hurry up before it doesn't ring anymore, noticing Charmin as the caller ID. I pick up the phone in style.

"Why, hello."

"Josh! Where are you?!"

"I'm at the house. Why? What's wrong?"

"It's Charles! He just got arrested and he's downtown!" Charmin yells frantically.

"Man what! What he do?!"

"I don't know, but me and Charm are going to pick you up in five minutes. Be ready."

"Okay," I say and hang up the phone, shocked and overwhelmed by the news. This has to be a mistake because Charles is the nicest, almost least intimidating person I know. Somebody must've lied.

I put on some better clothes to get ready and go downstairs to be prepared.

"Beep! Beep!" Their car blows outside. I hurry up to the car, so I can see what is really going on.

"Yo, how you found out about this?" I say as I hop in and close the door.

Charm drives off and says, "He called me from the station. He luckily knew my number by heart because if roles were switched, I don't think I would've known his number by heart."

"I can't believe it." I feel crushed on the ride.

"You okay?" Charmin puts her arm around my shoulder for comfort.

I look at her and say yes. We make it down to the station and walk in. It's nerve-wracking to be surrounded by policemen. I feel like if I sneeze too loud, I may get arrested on sight.

"Hello, we are here for Charles Woods."

The lady officer types on her computer and looks for Charles's information, hoping he can be released.

"I have Charles's information," the lady officer says.

"So why did he get arrested?"

"It says here that he was charged for assaulting a minor during a scuffle."

"What?!" Charmin exclaims. "Who made the charges?"

"It says here Sade Saddiq," she reads.

"Sade! Please ma'am, there has to be a mistake. This is all a lie," Charmin chimes.

"Well, the evidence is this video footage of him, throwing a minor in the air and hurting him."

"He was throwing him off of me!" I say with frustration. "Don't you see the minor hurting me and he comes to help me?"

"Sir, I do understand, but he could have broken the two of you apart without hurting him."

"OH MY GOD!" I erupt as an emotional wave takes over me. All the policemen notice my outburst, but I don't care. The knuck in me wanted to buck, but Charm makes sure I don't forget where I am at. The aura of the station breathes seize and control.

Charm says, "Is there a way we can get him out? Like a bail or something to pay?"

"No. He cannot be released unless Ms. Saddiq drops the charges."

"I can't believe that bitch," Charm says, reading my mind.

Together, we drive back home, ready to take over their trap they call a house. Why would she do that? I try to figure out the reason, but I don't understand as we pull up and park in front of her house. The renegade in me wants the smoke, but I know we can't afford to do anything after the fight and the party setup. Nowadays, I have to think about my decisions.

"Look," Charm says. "I will be more calm this time and there will be no fighting. Got it?"

"Yeah," Charmin and I agree.

"Josh, if you have anything to say, you can say it, but be respectful. Got it?"

"Yeah." I take a deep breath to contain all the fire that wants to ignite.

Charm leads the way to her doorstep as Charmin and I follow her. Once again, loud noises come from inside, but it sounds like Sade's voice talking on the phone. Charm triple rings the doorbell on purpose and we wait in patience. Sonny opens the door and he laughs in our faces, yelling, "Sade!"

"What?!" Sade says from the back of the house. Sade notices us and quickly hangs up on her phone as she walks up to us. "What y'all want?"

"I never thought this beef we have would get too far, but y'all done lost y'all minds putting Charles in jail. How could y'all?"

"No, how could y'all? Once again ya' little rascals here want to cause trouble and have Sonny not sell lemonade to the kids at the clubhouse anymore."

"That's his fault," I interject. "He wants to cheer on Rayland to call another girl a bitch."

"Who?" Sade says.

"Rayland. You know, little Rayland," Sonny says, showing his height with his hand.

"Ohh yeah, Rayland. That's family to us."

"No he's not!" I stomp his soul from my stare.

"Why yes he is, little Joshy," says Sonny, chuckling. "This is real funny, Sade. All year, this nigga would barely come out of his nest, talking to himself and now he wants to be out and about in the neighborhood. You still a weird, lame-ass nigga."

"Oh really?" I walk forward with all hands on deck to swing, but Charm stops me, moving me behind Charmin. Sonny laughs at the gesture.

"Look. I'm too old for this. So what do you want? What do you need so Charles can come home?"

Sade giggles. "Oh, Charm wants to fight for her man."

"We hear about y'all setting up the neighborhood clubhouse party on the 4th. Let Sonny sell his lemonade at the function and we will let him go the next day then," says Sonny.

"Pschtt! Oh hell naw, Charm. It has to be something else we can do. Charm don't do this," Charmin pleads. Hearing her proposition has me in the middle. My brother in jail is the problem, but Sonny's lemonade as the equalizer does not sit right with me. Plus, for him to be in there that long is cruelty.

Charm ignores her complaints, looking at me and Charmin for clarity. Charmin shakes her head in disagreement, but I give a hefty look, wishing that it didn't have to come to this, but nodding my head if it's the only way to get my brother back. A deal with the devil as I think about it.

Charm turns around and puts her hand out to shake. "Deal."

Sade shakes her hand and Sonny laughs his way back into the house as Charmin complains to Charm how she got played. Charm and Charmin go back and forth until they drop me off. As I walk off, Charmin says, "You can stay at our place if you want."

I think about it, but I say it's okay, feeling the pain of knowing he is in jail. Maybe when I come back to my senses, I'll regret saying no and slap myself. All I know as I walk into my four-corner room is that the summer can go either way from now on.

After a long day with the kids, I walk off with no discipline to take Rayland home and no enthusiasm to see Vickie work.

"Josh!" Speaking of Vickie, I turn back and see her jogging up to me.

"How are you doing? You okay?"

"Yeah I'm fine." I give my best smile to hide the pain.

"Well that's good. I know you are sad about Charles and so am I. I just want to let you know that I promise to finish the mural for him and when I'm done, you will be the first person to see it. Is that fine?"

"Yes, that's fine." I perk up as I know that will be special.

"Well, walk back safely and if you need anything, just let me know."

"Okay thanks." I walk back with more spirit. The reality sits in my heart, but I know it won't be for long. If Charles were here, he would want me to continue the party. It surprises that Vickie is willing to go into overtime with the mural instead of telling me to move the party to a later date. I guess she must've talked to Charles because the show must go on is his personality. I walk past Sonny's house with angst, but I try to control it. Some walks, I don't look at his house. Other times, I look at it and try to resist throwing a rock through the window or playing ding-dong ditch. Moving on, the mood transitions from hatred to strange when I walk past Old Man Williams' house. The atmosphere changes dramatically to where all the mosquitos want to attack me on the way home except when I walk past his house. Now that I think about it. I don't think I gave him a party flyer. The question is should I give him a flyer? Thinking about it, I say why not and make a u-turn to his doorstep. I grab the last flyer sheet out of my pocket, fold it, and slide it halfway underneath his door. Looking at it to make sure it is positioned neatly, the flyer sweeps inside from underneath and the door opens. I tremble backwards, staring to see what is inside while ready to run if anything pops out. The entry freezes me as I think about if I should walk in.

"Come in!" A loud, raspy voice speaks from what sounds like an outside speaker box. Catching my breath in agony, I walk in slowly, inspecting the inside with each step I take. The front of his house is decorated with pictures of him and his son and wife. In between each picture are his police awards, leading to a hanging police uniform on display. My steps take me into his living room where his big, flat screen is a large television with twenty camera screens of what looks like the neighborhood. The television scares as each screen has a camera bouncing back from each street. Old Man Williams scrolls in the room with his wheelchair attached to a railroad type track that transports him around the house.

"Well, are you going to stand there or sit down?" He points me to his plastic-wrapped couch. I take a seat, sinking heavily as I slide in the cushions. Old Man Williams scrolls his wheelchair next to me and we look at the screens on the television. Each screen is like a different channel. One screen is the Discovery Channel of the birds chirping and flying off the trees in one neighborhood. Another screen is the sports channel tuning in to the two-on-two basketball game at the clubhouse. Then another screen is Sonny walking to what looks like their house, which is next door.

"You know that boy?" he asks.

"Yeah," I say with agitation.

"He's a kid with a troubled past, but he's in big trouble."

"Why you say that?" I look at him with wonder.

"That kid is not himself right now. He's somebody else." He presses on the remote to flip back some videos. He turns to a video clip shot in the late spring where Sonny is chillin' at the clubhouse.

"Look at him," he says. Afro naps with his True Religion jeans and jays. I guess you can say he looks less evil. Just your normal dude. Old Man Williams flips forward to the more recent clips of him and then pauses.

"Now look at him." In this clip, he's at his lemonade stand with clean-cut Afro naps and a polo shirt. High-roller pants and plain shoes.

"What's the difference besides his look?" I say. He zooms in on his face to where we can see him closely and his eyes have a red shadow in his pupils. His smile is redder than normal color gums. Plus, his mustache has a more reddish tint than in the other clip.

"So do you know why he looks different?" I ask.

"I believe he has been taken in custody by a spirit."

"What do you mean? Why would you say that?" I'm shaking in my shoes as his tone gets deeper and the lights dim.

"So here's a story. Forty years ago, I was in this same house when the neighborhood was all white. My family and I never interacted with the neighborhood until I began selling lemonade. The lemonade was a success, bringing kids and adults to our house every year for a cup. One day, it was this red-head kid named Crosby, who loved to cause trouble, especially with my son. It seems like every other week was a story of how him and Crenshaw did this or Crenshaw did that, making us look bad. I always told him that he needs to find new friends besides Crosby. He was just a bad influence. So one day, I came home early from work and I walked into them smoking weed on our backyard patio. Crosby was passing him the joint after he puffed. I got so angry and told Crenshaw to go to his room and spanked Crosby so hard that he peed his pants."

I try to contain my laughter as his story continues, but I feel like the story gets interesting.

"After that, I took him to his parents' house and his parents beat him again. Plus, I think he was grounded for a whole summer." He looks at my flyer and changes his tone, chuckling as his dentures shine and clap together like dice. "Man, those parties were great times, son. Despite the racial tension and awkward conversations, those parties were the only time where I felt a part of the neighborhood and my lemonade was the shit! Sugar, honey and lemons, ice, tea; the shit!" he says, reminiscing about a happy time.

"So what happened?"

"It was the summer of '79 party. Rick James's Mary Jane song was blazin' that summer and at that party. I had everybody on cool because the sun was smoky that day. Crosby's parents wanted him to help me as a part of his punishment, so I did. I let him sell the lemonade while I went to go party and enjoy. During the midst of my dance, the DJ cuts the record, where Crosby is sprawled out on the ground with the lemonade spilled on his shirt. The parents call the ambulance to get him checked out while everyone talks about my lemonade and how they feel sick. Once he is gone and rumors spread, an uproar flips on me that my lemonade is the reason why he is at the hospital. Once he's pronounced dead by midnight, everyone assumed it was me and took me down. I begged, I pleaded, I did everything, but nobody would listen. It's crazy how nobody noticed how the lemonade was green when he sold it and how it was natural yellow originally."

"Yooooooo, Sonny's lemonade is green too!"

"That's my point, son. I believe the spirit of Crosby took over Sonny to where he contaminates the lemonade with marijuana and sells it to people."

"I knew it!" High-fiving my intuition. Oooo I can't wait to tell Charmin. "Wait, but he's gonna be selling the lemonade at the clubhouse party this upcoming 4th. What should I do?"

"That's fine. This is what I need you to do. Wear this necklace that day." I grab the old school medallion and find the crystal in the circle fascinating. "The only way to have his spirit disappear is get the whole neighborhood to come to the party, get his lemonade, and make a toast."

"The whole neighborhood?!"

"Did I stutter? Yes, the whole neighborhood. Then end the toast on 'to the soul of the neighborhood.' Once everybody cheers, things should be back to normal," says Old Man Williams, handing me the necklace. I grab it and put it in my pocket.

"Don't lose it now," he says as I walk over to his front door to leave.

Before I leave, I ask, "Are you gonna go to the party?"

Old Man Williams gives a grin and says, "I'll see what I can do."

I walk out in shock of all that took place. The walk home feels at ease as I think about the plan and wonder how I can get EVERYBODY in the neighborhood to come to the party and toast.

●⋯⋯⋯⋯●⋯⋯⋯⋯●

"Ooooo I got it," Charmin says with ease. I look at her with life's biggest answer.

"All we have to do is send an email that makes it mandatory for people to show up."

"That was your answer?" I say. Despite how I think her answer is basic, she has a point. We need to send something out that will make the least concerned person attend. Plus, it has to be where people show up on a good time. The party will be an all-day thing, but if everybody is there at the exact same time, then it will work.

"Help me brainstorm, Charmin. What is something that will get everybody to come to the party?"

Charmin and I think, blurting out anything that comes to mind.

"Free alcohol?"

"Yes, but from where?"

"Free shoes?"

"Yes, but once again from where?"

"Free weed?"

I look at Charmin in a facetious way. "Really Charmin? Free weed?"

"Mybad. You said to blurt out what comes to mind."

"See. We need something that will force everybody to come to the clubhouse. Like they need to come here before they do all their festive activities."

"Yeah," Charmin adds. "Like something before they do all their barbequing and cooking and firework stuff."

Thinking about what she said, her comments hit me declaring itself as the answer. "That's it, Charmin!"

"Whatchu' mean?"

"Let's do a mandatory pass that all neighbors need in order to barbeque or pop fireworks."

"Chill out, Josh. That's extreme. Plus, you think people are gonna abide by that law?"

"Well, that's where you come in," I say. Charmin looks at me in a peculiar way. "All the contacts Magic gave to you at the desk. Just hit one of them up for security and have them drive around the neighborhood for inspection."

"But that messes up Magic's budget."

"Then take it out of my budget," I say on the sly, hoping she doesn't hear me.

"Oh, so are you gonna take it out of your grass-cutting money?" Charmin asks. I look at her with little zeal to do so, but I hide my insecurity and take pride behind the words.

"Yeah, I'll do it."

"Okay. Let's do it then."

The next day after hangin' with the kids, I stay back after Zoe leaves to go home. One more day until the party and it is fresh on the minds of the kids. I pretend to clean up and move around things until Charmin comes to the clubhouse. As I wait, I sneak in the tarp to see Vickie work on the masterpiece for a little while. Serving two jobs with one brush and one spray can as she moves up and down the ladder with no monotonous muscle. I stand from afar and watch her work until I feel a hand on my shoulder, startling me as I turn around.

"Pschtt, Charmin!"

She laughs uncontrollably as we walk back into the clubhouse. She walks me to Magic's office and logs into his email. Watching her set up the format, I watch her write and I coach her along, making suggestions, proofreading and hitting the backspace as she types.

"Sincerely, Magic," Charmin finishes. I look at it and notice how she includes the key words that black people read for sincerity like "mandatory," "if not," and "federal law."

"Is it good?" Charmin asks. Reading more, I look over and check for clarity.

"Yeah it's good." I'm ready for Charmin to send it out. She counts out all the neighbors in our community and makes a list of the names as well. Charmin sends out the email to the neighborhood and prints out the list. Before we leave, we close the clubhouse and make sure Vickie is safe. We walk back together before Charmin departs to her house, excited for Thursday. I walk back to the house and pray for Charles. The celebratory antics for the Fourth becomes the least of my energy as I see the news. The neighborhood makes me feel like I'm in a country as a citizen where I feel patriotic to throw the party, sending out the air missiles and passing laws with emails. The president for a day with the fate of Charles in my hands.

The Clubhouse Party

What a beautiful day in the neighborhood as I wake up to an anticipated sensation for the day. Not just any day. A day for the neighborhood and the community where planning took a lot of days, but luckily, I have Charmin as the engine behind all the magic that will take place at the clubhouse. More magic than Disney World to where people will be captured by the music, the art, the spoken word, and the congregation of elation that flows in the air with our outside fans, cooling any heat and negativity that wants to perspire in the atmosphere. If it does, a drink from Sonny can help stall the taste buds to express any salt towards another before I make the toast and present the mural. A mural that has sweated behind the exertion of Vickie and shed tears behind the bad news of Charles. It will be a wonderful emblem to evoke unity and not just be a stain on the wall. After the festive toast, the good times will roll for people to hit the dance floor and let the vibrations take them to ecstasy, giving them energy to stay past the original closing. Plus, if any partygoer has one mission for the pass, then it will be facilitated by Magic, who Charmin convinced will be a good idea for regulation and party population purposes. One person I hope to see is Old Man Williams due to his legacy and his unsung role to shut down Sonny's bad influence, so he can release Charles. After the cleanup and coming back with Charles, life will be normal.

I go down to the clubhouse early and go along with the instructions of Charmin as she points Magic to set up the orange cones for the entrance and points in a direction for me to put the chairs.

"Let's go, people." She directs us as if she is Debbie Allen on a movie set. The bossiness throws me off as I want to tell her to do something, but I guess I can play my role. The clubhouse turns into a complete set for fun with each room inside for different people to play games and cards. The open area where Zoe and I look after the kids are for the Drink My Paint group except Vickie's close friend, Trischa, will be over it. The court outside will be filled with people to play team basketball to where I will handle the teams and mix in young kids and teenagers to play a good game. The mural will be tarped and security will have it protected as the playground in front of it will be with little ones as Vickie may watch them from time to time. Charmin makes her demands, but deep down she worries for the DJ and the S.T.C group since they will be performing before the mural. She walks around, running the show, but hopes to have a spring in her step and her jump when it's her time to perform. The stage setup is small, but has enough for them to do their routine as the DJ's set and speakers are on wheels. He will be outside with the music in the day and then roll his music inside during the night. The realm of a space looks complete as every station, every set, and every piece of this puzzle of a party comes together. As I sit down to observe people walk in, I see Sonny walk in with his cooler and equipment. He chats to Magic for a second upon entrance and walks up to me, but I pay him no mind and look at the kids on the playground.

"Magic says you have to tell me where to set up."

I look at a good area so the plan for every person to have his lemonade works. Magic stands near the cones of the entrance and a piece of the sidewalk has a little space for him to set up and be a part of the view as they walk in. Looking at his stuff and measuring the width and length of his area, I know he can squeeze there.

"Go over there." I point near the entrance. He says okay and struggles to go over as he holds the table in one hand while rolling his cooler. I would help him, but he'll be okay. I make my way over too once the DJ sets the tone for the day, playing Summertime by DJ

Jazzy Jeff & Fresh Prince as the first song to commence the party. The song blazes across the air, triggering more people to come as I walk away from a line of people coming in. Bouncing my way over to the basketball court, I see Rayland shooting by himself. I run over to join him, intercepting his rebound after he shoots a brick.

"Wassup Rayland?" I say, figuring out how to dribble the ball with both hands. I shoot my jumper with the little form I try to imitate and it misses, landing in the grass. Rayland goes over to get it and comes back to dribble. Guarding him as he shoots, I see a plethora of kids leave their mothers and run over to the court to play. After Rayland makes his shot, another kid takes his ball, not abiding by the make it-take it rules, and goes off with it. He dribbles off on the other side of the court as kids chase him, prowling for the ball. The kid goes up for the lay up and the cycle continues back and down the court where Rayland chases to get his ball. I try to join in, but I get quadruple teamed every time I get the rebound. Hounding me for the ball when I try to dribble, stealing my shine before I can go. I get off to the side and watch them play, wishing for a little ounce of their extra energy. The kids take no breaks for thirty minutes. It's just all play. No referee or rules to street ball. Anything goes. Watching them from the side, I see from a distance a local crew of teenagers walk over after leaving their girlfriends. A group of "monstars" in appearance. Big and mean. They look ready to ball. Ignoring court etiquette of getting next, they walk in the game of the little kids and disrupt their flow.

"Heyyy! What are y'all doing?" Rayland asks one of the guys. A tall dude with a white T-shirt, who looks big in physique and athletic with his retro Jordans.

"We takin' over. Get off the court and watch the big boys play."

The kids get mad and walk off the court in disappointment, but Rayland stays to play.

"Didn't you hear what I say?" the guy says. Rayland ignores him and continues to play, shooting layups in the midst of their game. The guy comes off, grabs Rayland's rebound, and throws his ball on the grass disrespectfully. I see the event and I walk over to address the problem, feeling like the new sheriff in town with some power in my hands.

"Aye yo, bro. You can't do that to the little kids. They were here first. If you want to play, you can play on that end and they can play on that end."

The guy hears me and continues to pass it to one of his guys, laughing at my address. The disrespect times two. I compose myself, knowing Rayland and the kids are watching so I just think of a better plan. The boys continue to play with each other, tipping in each other's shots, making acrobatic passes for the dunk finish until I grab the rebound and throw their ball off the court way past the grass, rolling in the woods. The guys get mad and walk up to me as a gang, ready to beat me up, until the plethora of kids walk up behind me, game face on for any action. Poised and composed for the smoke. I wish I was that hard as a kid. Seeing them back off, I tell Rayland to go get both of the balls and bring them to me. Rayland runs over to get them. The guys pout in their stances, mad at the situation. Once he brings me the basketballs, I look them in their faces hard.

"Abide by the rules of the court or you will be escorted by the security up front to leave. Y'all feel me?"

The guys shake their heads as I start the fun with my shot as the tip-off for the kids and my pass to the "monstars" to play on the other side of the court. As soon as I try to play, I get a call from Charmin, feeling the urgency as it rings in my pocket.

"Hello?"

"Hey, go to the spoken word room to start it off. I got a neighbor who referees on the side to come down."

"Okay," I say, hanging up and walking over. Before I make it to the clubhouse, Rayland comes over to hug me and says thank you, smiling with joy. I walk back to the clubhouse with love and sentiment, developing happy feelings that I need to express on the mic. Maybe my piece can be called Happy Feelings. I go inside the clubhouse and walk through the love of women at tables talking, men sipping lemonade like 4th of July beer, and little kids running around getting on somebody's nerve. When I enter the spoken word room, kids are napping through the words of somebody talking on the microphone. An early morning schoolteacher and his children. Both are not ready to welcome each other. More people get up to go and it turns into a boredom convention. Something needs to change and I know the spoken word is not turning into the best idea. Think, Josh, think! I crawl into my little hole in my brain and get sidetracked as the DJ plays the Show, having me bop to the beat, ready to drop a verse on the beat.

"That's it!"

I take out my phone and call Charmin to bring me her mini speaker. She becomes all suspicious for why I need it, but I tell her to trust me. Hanging up the phone with sass, she comes over in a long ten minutes, making me want to go off because it takes her forever; however, I am cool as a reminder. I grab the clubhouse laptop and connect it to the speaker, logging on YouTube and searching for beats. A modern Langston Hughes finishes his piece, making the majority kid audience fall out on their crystal stairs called lives. I clap with volume to awake the energy and I go up on the stage to talk.

"That was great, guys. What we are going to do right now is a switch-a-roo with the spoken word and put it on a beat." All the kids make confused faces, wondering what is going on. I hurry to the laptop to look up an instrumental and play it.

"Boom-tap, Boom-baboom-tap, Boom-tap, Boom-baboom-tap!"

Kids perk up as they wonder what I am about to rap. I feel nervous, hoping to not fail. Clearing my throat for a concise voice, I close my eyes once the beat drops and then rap as if I'm blind to the critique of the audience. I hear laughs as I rap and bop, feeling the vibe, but not seeing the vibe.

"Here I go, here I go. Looking through your window." Probably the hardest line I say all rap.

In the rap, I am a blind boy, laughing at the lyrics that I am saying. I rock out like a cold MC, but lyrically rap as if I'm reading a

Dr. Seuss book. Continuing into midflow, a little kid comes on stage to save me. He grabs the microphone and says I got this, rocking the crowd from the jump. Charmin and a bunch of girls walk in and stop to hear, amazed at the little kid's rhyme. A little Casanova in style. Cornrows with a smile to match, he has the star power and he wins over the audience easily with his swag. Every head nods and bops with him, vibing to his flow. Once the YouTube beat stops, he continues to flow acapella style while little kids clap their hands to keep it going. No music doesn't hurt nobody. I stand on the stage and hype him up. The little kid finishes with a crowd-pleasing bar, which leaves everybody in shambles after he drops the mic. Whoops and hollers from fans across the room. Charmin comes up to the stage and tells everybody to come out for the S.T.C dance performance. All the kids jump in excitement and run out of the room. Charmin walks slowly as everybody leaves.

"You ready?" I say.

"I hope so." She takes her time as she walks out. It surprises me in a funny way because this is the first time I will see her perform. The crowd of people walks out as well, setting the stage for a big audience. As we walk to the stage, Charmin goes to a car to change her wardrobe. I wait in hysteria, picturing how she is gonna show out. Charm walks up first, decked out in her '90s Aaliyah flannel and top with leggings and black shoes. Tiffany and Charmin come from behind her ten minutes later with the same look with shades to match. My eyes are stunned by the attire, locking in my cheeks to not blush because I am in love right now. A fan of hers off the rip, I try to control my groupie hormones and be cool, paying attention to watch Magic introduce them to the crowd.

"Please give it up for S.T.C.!!!!!!!!!!" The crowd claps as the group takes their places on stage. The DJ waits for his number and plays No Cap Nate. Once the kids hear the song, they get hype ready to see the performance. As I'm waiting for them to start, No Cap Nate comes from behind me and jogs his way out stage with the group, surprising me with his three Cuban links appearance. Charm leads the choreography on stage, jigging behind him as he raps and sings. The crowd is into him; even the older people bop their head from time to time. The stage becomes electric as the group circles themselves around him as he breaks it down to the crowd. Bouncing on their toes, Charm comes out of the circle and begins flipping her ass off once the song's bridge starts, landing and bouncing again like a pogo stick. The kids woah over her. Jumping up and down screaming over her hops. Tiffany sways in next, pop-n-lockin' until it's time to show the crowd what she's working with. She turns around and twerks it out. As No Cap Nate continues his verse, he jumps right in and gets behind to dance. The crowd cheers them on as the dance goes along with the beat.

"Here we go(ayyye!) Here I go(ayyye!) There she go(ayyye!) It's a go(ayyyye!)"

Little girls scream in excitement, throwing their hands out for No Cap Nate. He sees one girl, falling out, screaming to get a touch. He goes over there, rapping his hook and grabs her hand, pulling her to come on stage. All the girls scream next to her in pandemonium.

"Ohhhh My God!!!!"

He pulls her on stage, letting security know it's okay. He then takes her next to him, dancing together as Charmin gets ready to jump in. She comes bouncing on her toes, doing the Scotch. She hops it out and does a flip with a bunny hop, inviting the crowd to try it, which you jump and pull your feet to your hands. The little kids try, showing the older people how. No Cap Nate sings the instructions too. I peep Magic on the other side, doing his best to coordinate himself to the movement and beat. The flow doesn't look right on him. Charmin grooves her way back to the circle and the ladies huddle in towards him and finish with a pose, making everybody cheer for applause. No Cap Nate runs off the stage and walks past me, smiling as a hello. Then S.T.C comes to me, high-fiving and hugging each other. Charmin gasps for air and smiles at my reaction to their performance. "How did you think I did?"

"You were lit!!!" Bouncing on my toes, I try to do the Scotch and bunny hop.

Laughing, she says, "Okay now I see you." Noticing the sweaty faces, I go off the stage to grab some towels. As I'm walking down the stairs of the stage, Sade walks up, bombarding past the stage manager, heated about the performance. I notice and make a quick u-turn and call for backup.

"So all along you wanted to shake ya ass on No Cap Nate. Ain't that some shit?" Sade says, launching herself at Charm. Security grabs her as she tries to scruffle off of them.

"You ain't shit, Charm. You and your bitch-ass sister. That's why y'all niggas suck," she yells while a few good security men escort her off stage. S.T.C doesn't faze the hate as they continue to celebrate with themselves. No Cap Nate comes back out to talk to them.

"Yoooo! Y'all ladies were dope."

"Thank you," Charm says while Tiffany and Charmin cheese.

"I know we got dancers for my music video, but I got a performance at the Epicenter in a couple weeks and I would love for y'all to perform with me."

The group looks toward each other, screaming in synchronicity. Charm calms herself down first and makes the decision. "Yes. That will be nice."

"Great," he says. "Give me your number and my people will be in contact with you."

Charm exchanges numbers and the group bounces in a frenzy, not believing what just happened. Magic looks at me and gives me the cue that the toast will be happening in the next ten minutes.

"Okay bet." I look at Charmin and tell her to go change quick. I go off the stage to see the list of people who are to make sure everybody is here. Only one person is missing. Wheeling himself to me is him. Old Man Williams walking and smiling with a pipe in his mouth.

"It's about that time, sir."

"Okay. Let me get this cup and I will take my place," he says, rolling his way to Sonny's.

I notice how most of the people get ready to go back to their event stations, so I run on stage.

"Ummmm excuse me?" Everybody turns around to wonder what is going on.

"In the next five minutes, we will need everybody to come gather in this area for a neighborhood toast. The cups are at Sonny's Lemonade stand. Once you get a cup, come back and we will get started right away. Thank you." The wave of the crowd shifts in the direction of Sonny. Magic comes up to me and gives me a cup. I look out from the side of the stage as everyone indulges in Sonny's Lemonade. It bothers me, but I know today will be his last lottery day sale. Sonny continues to pass out the cups as people walk over to me. I see people sip a little, just to feel the sweet taste. Lips smack and more sips take place as people congregate over to me. Old Man Williams is the last in line, ready to get his cup.

Oh no! I think. "Charmin! Go over there and get Old Man Williams' cup for him."

"Why? He's right there in line."

"Just do it. Now!" I say with no cap on my face. Charmin hurries over there and gets a cup before Old Man Williams can meet Sonny face to face. I give her a signal to turn him around immediately and walk him to the crowd. She throws a thumbs-up and does it. That's my girl. The DJ passes over the time with music to continue the conversations that have nothing else to say. Magic comes to the stage to conduct the crowd and grabs their attention.

"Excuse me! Excuse me! My beautiful neighbors, excuse me! May I have your attention please?!" The people begin to lower their volume and turn to the attention of Magic.

"If I didn't tell you when you came in, hear me clearly. Welcome to Mountain Oaks neighborhood clubhouse party. We appreciate every one of you for coming. So many things you could've been doing for your Fourth of July and you chose to be with us. Me and the Mountain Oaks association staff want you to enjoy yourselves today and understand how we are each other's keeper. It takes a village to raise a child and it takes a village to make a safe haven. We as a people endure a lot from the outside. Negativity and simple-minded thoughts of what people say we are. Today is a reminder for the community that we are a family and that we create the environment for love and change. With that being said, I'm going to have one of our own come to the stage. He had the idea to bring back the clubhouse party and he has a few words and a toast to elevate your day. After the toast, we will move to the playground area in front of the wall to unveil the new mural. Please give a warm welcome to Josh Woods!"

The crowd claps for me as I walk to the microphone shaking. Magic gives me a handshake and I look across the crowd nervous by the size. The one time I want to close my eyes and I can't. I find myself stuck to where voices clear and eyes look, wondering if I will talk. I take a deep breath and begin.

"Once again thank you all for coming," I say clearing my throat. "It's really a testament to the love you have for this community. It's funny because I didn't start to love this community until this summer. All it took was a grass-cutting job and a little of Sonny's juice to make me feel the love." I point to him in a shoutout. He looks over and makes a strange face in confusion.

"This neighborhood is beautiful. Not because of the aesthetics of the tall oak trees and the park by the neighborhood, but the people that encompass this neighborhood. We have our ups and downs as people, but we need to get back positivity and uplift each other the right way. The houses we live in are houses, but the community we live in is home to where it is comfortable to come back home after we leave and put our stamp on the world. So everybody, lift up this good lemonade and let's toast." Everybody lifts up their cup in respect, moved by my words.

"Let's toast to happiness and positivity as a community. To the soul of the neighborhood!" I say, raising my cup.

"To the soul of the neighborhood!" The crowd raises their cups and drinks. I feel a cosmic spirit enter and tremble the necklace, where the bad chakras emit into the medallion piece of the necklace. Once the trembling stops around my neck, I drink and a disgusting taste fills my mouth, causing me to make a sour face as I look upon the crowd for their reaction. I pinpoint people who are doing the same thing, except for Old Man Williams, who smiles at me with a thumbs-up.

"Now let's head over to the unveiling of the mural," I conclude.

The neighborhood people head over to the playground area. A lot of kids and people throw away their cups with the rest of the juice left. Sonny sees the reactions and is confused by them. Charmin and I meet up with Sonny as he processes the sour responses of the juice. We tell him that he needs to go get my brother out of jail now. Not tonight, not tomorrow, but now. In a disappointed mood, he agrees and leaves. Charmin and I walk over together, proud and relieved. The DJ walks with us while he carries the microphone and two speakers to the playground area in front of the covered-up mural. Vickie comes in front of the people while the kids look from the tops of the playground and the adults look from the ground.

"Hey, guys. My name is Victoria Monet. I have been a resident here for eight years and I love how involved we are as a community, especially in the arts. I run my own nonprofit organization called Drink My Paint and we support paint-n-sip parties for community kids. When the opportunity came to me to paint a mural for the community, I knew I needed help and I needed inspiration. I got in touch with another resident named Charles Woods, Josh's brother, and we came together to give you a special piece. The inspiration comes from a Langston Hughes poem called I, too. A nice poem that talks about how America neglects certain groups in representation. In honor of the 4th of July, we did a piece that speaks to inclusivity, diversity, and unity. Drum roll please." The DJ plays a drum roll audio and the tarp comes down.

"Wowwwwwwwwwwwww," everyone says, glued to the picture that can never be televised. A vase glassing in an exotics bouquet of different flowers. The type of flowers that came from different parts of the country and maybe the world. Inside the vase has a couple of kids holding each other's hand behind a house. One kid is black. The other kid is white and the other kid is Hispanic. The majority of the neighborhood's population are these ethnicities. Staring at it for a long time, I just look at the vibrant colors and how it bounces off the wall. Any kid can come to the clubhouse and play on the playground while the mural talks to you. The love and unity of the kids sprouts the flowers in the vase, showing a sign of where the neighborhood needs to get back to. Residents form a line to take pictures as kids play near it as the piece looks down on them. The DJ brings his set inside as some people continue to work around the clubhouse. The rest of the day turns into a matrix of joy for people to dance and talk. The signature of Vickie and Charles complements the piece, bringing me joy to my brother's name on the wall. He would be speechless to see how the neighborhood loves the mural.

"How you like it?" Charmin asks, walking over to me.

"I love it," I say with sentiment, wishing Charles was here.

"Let's go to the dance floor. Let's see if you can Scotch."

"Okay."

I walk inside and to the dance floor with Charmin. She starts to feel me when I show her my hops and my jigs, making it a fun time. In mid-dance, Old Man Williams wheels into me, pulling me to the side.

"Good job today. Without you, the neighborhood would be the same, so good job, boy."

"No problem," I say, giving him a firm hug. I give him his necklace back and he moves on with a bounce in his crutch. I turn around to get back into my groove and then I feel another tap on the shoulder. I turn around and it's Charles.

I jump on him with no instinct. All the feelings manifested from him being gone took over me and I couldn't control it. Tearing up a little.

"Bro, I thought you were gone for a minute."

"Man I know, but it's all good. I'm just glad to be home."

"Yeah, bro. You need to tell me about how it is in jail."

Charles flies past that subject and says, "We can talk about that later, but bro, you look different."

I giggle from his comments. "What do you mean?"

"I don't know. I know I was gone for a minute, but you look different," he says.

"I don't know about that, but I feel good. Today was a success and you're back, so I guess my joy is shining today." Charles embraces me. A cool big brother moment I would've never imagined.

"Oh yeah. One more thing," says Charles, waving Sonny to come over our way. He walks over as if he looks more like the one that came out of jail.

"Hey bro, I know all the shit I've done and the crazy shit I've started and I just want to say I'm sorry. You and your brother are cool. I was just trippin.'"

"I appreciate that. Me and Charmin are sorry too. We never meant to stop your hustle. We just let something small turn to something that shouldn't have been big."

"I gotchu, bruh. We cool?" Sonny says, giving his hand out. The outcome of this moment happening was zero to zero about an hour ago, but I give.

"Yeah we cool." We dap it up and keep it cool.

Charmin and I party the rest of the night and decide to clean up the next day. It takes us a long time to clean up, but we try our best to do it. Charmin brings Missy over to watch her as we clean up. Magic comes over and thanks me for my job well done and decides we should do this every year. I say thank you and he gives me a cup of juice. I sit down at a nearby table and decide to take my break. As I sit my cup down, Charmin comes and grabs it.

"Give me my juice," I say.

"Mybad. Let me get a sip."

"Naw that's nasty." I say, straining over and around her to get my cup back.

"You scared of the cooties?"

"Hell yeah," as I finally find the reach and get a hold of my cup.

Charmin sits down next to me and makes the same face she's been dropping all summer.

"Look, I just wanted to say thank you. You really did make this happen. When we go back to school, we need to do more stuff like this. Like for real. Stuff like this. Together," she says with an emphasis on that last word.

"Yeah that's cool with me."

"Good. So I don't know if you know, but we might be with No Cap Nate at the Epicenter in a couple weeks. We supposed to perform and everything. That same weekend is the new Summer Juice movie coming out and I was wondering if you would like to go with me?" She fiddles her hoop earring. I keep it cool by not saying anything. A stone-cold face as I shake the juice in my cup like I didn't hear the question. Sometimes, I think girls like that play-hard-to-get act.

"Well?" Charmin asks with emphasis. I look at her as if I'm mesmerized by this juice and by her question.

I get up and say yes, leaving her for a quick second to get some more of that juice, wishing I could savor that taste for the rest of the summer.

About the Author:

Jonathan Wynn is a current player in the National Football League. He plays defensive end and is going into his third year with the Detroit Lions. Off the field, he lives up to his #AthleteAnd campaigns by prospering in creative endeavors, such as, running a clothing line called You Know I'm Prolly and being an avid writer in his spare time.

Growing up in Stone Mountain, Georgia, Jonathan was an active kid that loved to play outside and watch television. His imagination ran wild with numerous Christmas sing-a-longs made with his sister, living room performances in front of his parents, and classic daydreams when he was done running around. For him, a lot of daydreams came and went, but more daydreams came and happened as he grew up. The dream of playing football on the highest stage started with a lovely career at his high school alma mater, Stephenson High School. Jonathan became a top recruit and was granted a scholarship to attend Vanderbilt University. There, he played great SEC football in the wonderful city of Nashville, turning himself into a great player and a Vanderbilt man, graduating with a B.S. degree in 2017.

Double majoring in Educational Studies and History, Jonathan did not begin to flex his writing muscle until his senior year, coming up with stories and sharing his ideas with peers. Once it appeared to him that he was a good writer and creative, he put his ideas into action. He began writing the short story of "Summer Juice" in 2019 during his second-year in the NFL, and while selling his clothing line on the side.

Following a memorable 2019 season, Jonathan continues to write, create, and play football, utilizing all his seeds that God has blessed him to have in 2020.

Connect with Jonathan Wynn on Social Media

Instagram: @wayyback_wynn

Facebook: Jonathan Wynn

Twitter: @Eat_Grind_Wynn

www.ingramcontent.com/pod-product-compliance
Lightning Source LLC
Chambersburg PA
CBHW060800210726
48292CB00013B/1523